"When they found I was reading this, the nurses at my Swiss sanitorium took it away. (I won't tell you what I did to get it back, but there was no long-term damage.)"
    - Abigail Critchley

"I used to like Capri. And Cape Hatteras. And London."
    - Morris Quint

"I suppose there's something here a sophomore English class might like."
    - Matthew Ryan, Headmaster, Adams Hall

"What kind of people *have* you been meeting?"
    - The author's mother

ISBN: 9798650509370

Thoughts and Whispers
Tales of More Undivulged Crimes

by

Michael Reidy

Lattimer & Co.

PHILADELPHIA • LONDON • PARIS

2020

For Kerry & Sally

. . .the people muddied,
Thick and unwholesome
in their thoughts and whispers. . . .
- Hamlet, IV, v

Foreword

The tales in *Thoughts and Whispers* follow those in *Undivulged Crimes* in that they were written over a similar time-span and are set in Europe and the United States.

Four of the tales are labelled "Westbury Tales." They are united in their setting in a fictitious Massachusetts city that is a composite of places like Lawrence, Lowell, Springfield, Worcester, and other former manufacturing centers in New England. Cities like Westbury have had to reinvent themselves since the post-World War II migration of industry. Westbury also features in *The Rock Pool* and *Ardmore Endings*.

As in *Undivulged Crimes*, the central question is, "What do you really know about those around you?" Speculating on what they might be capable of is unsettling as the various innocent heroes and heroines of these stories reluctantly learn.

July 2020
In self-isolation.
It doesn't matter where.

Contents

x

The Hayride
A Westbury Tale

Thoughts and Whispers

The Hayride
A Westbury Tale

Autumn 1966

The clocks had been turned back the previous weekend and the darkness closed in on the afternoon. Cold huddles of shoppers and students waited impatiently for their buses under the large marquee across the front of Dexter's department store.

Bright lights shone down on the crowds, and large plate glass windows, already hinting at Christmas, cast a warm glow into the cold night.

Above the chatter rose the roar of dirty diesel buses, hissing their airbrakes and lumbering off to their destinations with steamy windows.

"In front of Dexter's" was the place for assignations. Ladies would meet to begin their shopping; businessmen would meet there to decide where to go for lunch; and between 3:30 and 5:30, students from the Westbury's schools would meet to change buses on the way home. It was a particular meeting place for the boys from the Academy and the girls from Pinehill. Many had known each other and their families from previous schools, or through other connections like church, dancing classes or music lessons.

They met as part of a routine that seemed to fill their youth.

John and Nick had known each other most of their lives and consequently shared many friends who frequented the Saturday night parties and dances. John was the more academically clever of the two, but Nick had an easy cosmopolitan manner that compensated for having inaccurate information. Both boys were popular, thought to be interesting and possessed one or two individual accomplishments.

It was on that Thursday after the clocks went back, while they were waiting in front of Dexter's, that they met Sally Hawes with a girl they did not know.

Sally and the girl walked into the light under the marquee and saw John and Nick standing along the window, about twenty feet away. They stopped at the far window and appeared to study the display.

John looked at Nick as if to say, "Do we want to talk to them?" Nick by way of answer picked up his book bag and they walked over to the girls.

"It's pretty slinky," said the girl they did not know, looking at the dress on the manikin. "I don't think I could ever wear anything like that."

"Are the buses running late?" asked Sally, turning to John.

Unlike many of the girls from Pinehill, Sally continued to wear her uniform properly when off campus. She always looked good, but it was an effortless look, unlike the look of the new girl.

"You haven't met Josie, have you?" Sally asked. "She's my cousin from Arizona. She's come to Pinehill for a few weeks while my aunt and uncle are away."

"Hi, Josie," John and Nick said.

"Do you boys think that dress is too slinky?" Josie asked.

Josie had a round face with bright blue eyes and dark blonde hair. She was taller than Sally and looked awkward in her uniform, as if she were wearing someone else's.

"I think it's a pretty hot dress," said Nick.

Josie looked doubtful, but Sally chirped, "That's what I told her."

"I just don't know what sort of thing I'd wear a slinky dress like that to."

"There are lots of parties coming up," John said.

"It would be great for the Holly Ball," Nick said.

John looked to the corner where the buses came around. Lights of cars stretched out in both directions, barely moving. Among the crowds crossing the street, John saw two familiar figures approaching.

Stu Gardner and Buzz Keogh were students at St Benedict's which was on another hilltop, a few miles away.

Nick and John knew Stu and Buzz from junior high

school. Well known for antics and escapades, they were frequently in trouble, but it was never serious. They had exuberant natures and ready smiles, Stu playing the straight man to Buzz's innovative anarchy.

"A party already!" Buzz said, as they joined the others.

"We're just in time, Stu. Wouldn't that be a great idea?" he extemporized, focusing on Josie, whom he had not met before. "We should organize a party one afternoon, right here. Get the whole gang down after school, have a ton of food, music, and dance with people when they tried to get on the bus."

Josie glanced at Sally, not knowing whether this was an old friend or the town drunk.

"This is my cousin, Josie," Sally said. "This is Stu and Buzz. I've known them forever," she said ambiguously.

"Hi, Josie," said Stu. "Is that short for Josephine?"

"No, it's the standard length for Josie," Sally interrupted.

"That was great, Josie," Buzz exclaimed looking at her closely. "I didn't see your lips move at all."

Josie gave a snorting laugh, then quickly covered her mouth and snorted again.

"Not from around here?" Buzz said with a long lazy drawl.

"A bit further west," Nick said.

Buzz and Stu looked at Josie as though examining a

specimen of unknown life. She laughed and snorted again.

"Arizona," she said when she recovered.

"Arizona," said Buzz, musing. "I've heard of that. It's a real place, is it?"

Sally moved from Josie and began talking to Nick and John. John focused on Sally, but Nick watched Stu and Buzz. They were asking her questions, telling her about the latest prank they were planning and asking what she thought of New England.

"It's like the movies," Josie said. "All the houses look like a toy village – and they're so old. There aren't a lot of trees where I'm from – well, not very near me – so everything feels really different. I'm – " she checked herself.

"What is it?" Nick asked, joining their conversation. "Nothing," said Josie.

"I know what it is," said Sally. "Josie doesn't really like the closed in feeling with all the trees."

"Never mind," said Buzz generously. "It's probably how'd we'd feel in a jungle."

"Or a cave," said Stu.

Sally absently looked up the street as a bus came around the corner.

"Damn! It's a twenty-one."

"Whoa! That's ours!" said Buzz trying to sound like Yosemite Sam. "Come on, Gabby," Stu said, "or we'll miss the chuck wagon."

Josie laughed easily because there was absolutely no malice in the way they carried on.

"One of the damn coach horses threw a shoe yesterday," Buzz continued. "Luckily, the Wells Fargo wagon was a-comin' – "

"Adios, Josie," Stu called over his shoulder as he shoved Buzz towards the bus. "If we end up on ponies again because you've been chewing the fat with the fillies – "

His voice was drowned out by the bus revving its engine, and they jumped up the stairs and the doors flapped shut.

Josie was laughing, and gave a wave to the bus, but its windows were too dirty to see inside.

"Josie!" Sally exclaimed at the openness of her approbation.

"They're funny," she giggled.

"They're idiots!" Sally said definitely.

Josie looked at Nick, who, with the merest hint of a smile, nodded towards Sally. The four of them looked at each other in silence for a moment, then Nick spoke.

"What do you think of Pinehill?" he asked.

With Josie under control again, Sally stepped away from the group, ostensibly to look for another bus, but Nick got the feeling it was because she knew Josie's answer and didn't like it.

"It's different," Josie said.

Nick was about to press her for a more detailed answer when Sally came back.

"Here's the bus," she said.

Josie collected her bags from where they leaned against the building. "Are you two going to Patricia's party Saturday?" Sally asked.

"Yes," John said. "She asked us yesterday."

The bus rolled to a noisy, smoky stop and the doors flapped open with a sharp hiss.

"Come on, Josie," Sally called. "We'll see you there."

"Will Buzz and Stu be there?" Josie asked.

Sally took her by the arm and they hauled their bags up the steps and took a seat. Josie looked out the window, but Sally fussed with her coat and books. Josie looked at John, gave a small wave and smiled.

Another loud, deep diesel roar and a flashing of lights and a billow of smoke and the bus moved off into the darkness.

଼

Patricia Detweiler's house, though not far from John and Nick's, was in a neighborhood where houses were stone and brick, not shingle and clapboard. It sat back from the street, and a perfectly manicured and leafless expanse of lawn separated it from the real world. It was a long building and the top two floors had gabled windows and the ivy that clung to the walls gave it a fairy tale appearance.

Lights glowed from most of the windows and white smoke issued from two of the chimneys.

"I love that smell," said Nick as they approached. "Cold clear nights and the smell of a wood fire."

"A good night for a party," John agreed.

The door was opened for them by Patricia's mother who greeted them warmly. She had known them since they were about four, and when Patricia was just a girl and not as beautiful as she was now.

"I'm so glad you boys could come. Old friends are important to have and keep," Mrs. Detweiler said.

"There are people just about everywhere. You know your way around, but be sure to go up to the study. Mr. Detweiler, I am sure, would like to see you."

Magnus Detweiler's family had started one of the town's largest industries in the early 1800s and it had been run by their descendants ever since.

As Patricia was the only one of her generation in the family, what happened next to Detweiler, Harris & Finn was the subject of continuing speculation. The Harrises and Finns had long since died out. Sale to an out of town buyer looked most likely, though the possibility of Patricia marrying someone able to take over – and produce further heirs – was judged to be preferable.

This fact was well known by people well beyond the Detweiler's friends, and it was enough to prevent Patricia from having any steady boyfriends – yet. Everyone she knew was a native who looked forward to escaping his hometown, but once she got to college, the equation would change.

Patricia herself had come to reflect these expectations in her appearance, so despite her pretty blonde looks. She carried an air of acceptance that only those who had known her for a long time understood.

John and Nick had watched Patricia through the years and noted that she seemed to grow quieter and more resolved as she grew older. Nevertheless, she was attractive and fun, and my friends liked her and her parents who always welcomed us.

John and Nick routinely discussed the people they knew and the interesting ones were naturally discussed at greater length. Like most interesting people, Patricia was an anomaly. Though seemingly incapable of defending herself, she defended her friends and acquaintances with a resoluteness that one would not expect. She railed against unkindness, thoughtlessness and injustices, no matter how small. She was a fiercely loyal friend who was not afraid of supporting an underdog.

For all that, a steady boyfriend eluded her. Both John and Nick had taken her to parties and dances, and she had been out with them as often as with anyone. All they could conclude was that she was waiting for a destiny that she knew did not live near home.

John and Nick headed towards the back of the house where there was a large room that opened onto the garden in warm weather. Tonight, the curtains were drawn and warm lights, an open fire and candles made it one of the best rooms they knew.

Patricia stood there in a striking red dress handing cups of cider to people.

Josie was with her, dressed more casually in a sweater and skirt. She was talking animatedly and reached her punch-line just as Nick and John came into hearing.

Patricia laughed with Josie and greeted us.

"Thank you for coming," she said. "Have you met Josie? She's just been telling me about some of her friends back home. It's good to have someone new in the crowd."

"I wish Sally thought so," said Josie to no one in particular.

As at most parties, there was dancing and food and the sort of chat that people thought was appropriate at parties. Some was clever, some was pretentious, some was mean, and some was very, very earnest.

The company was fluid as it is with old friends, and John and Nick found time to talk to nearly everyone.

"Are you going on the hayride?" someone asked near the end of the party. "Yes, I want to," said Nick, " but I haven't asked anyone yet."

The hayride was *the* November event. It was run by the Academy and Pinehill as a joint event and the Pinehill girls reckoned that if they had a date for the hayride, they'd have an escort for the Holly Ball at Christmas which was nearly as important as the prom.

Homecoming was nice, but not essential to social standing, whereas the Holly Ball was crucial. The hayride was the ideal time to coax an invitation.

The Homecoming dance was in the school gym – only the Academy had a homecoming – and the hayride culminated in an informal meal of hamburgers, corn on the cob, cider and pumpkin pie in a barn, while the Holly Ball was in a hotel downtown of 1920s elegance, bright lights and tasteful decorations, a good band and a dance floor crowded with smartly dressed people.

Sally had gone on the hayride – and to the Holly Ball – with John the previous year and was looking forward to a return engagement, even though he had taken Amy Armitage to the Junior Prom. That had been unforgivable as the two were acting in the school play together at the time. Well, even if John didn't take her, there was Nick.

Nick had taken Cindy Davis out all last year, Sally remembered. But, quite suddenly in the early summer, things had gone wrong, and Cindy and her family had moved a away. Nick had never heard from Cindy again which he didn't understand, and consequently, never talked about.

There were stories, but few people believed them.

"What happens on a hayride?" Josie asked, as the remaining guests sat on the floor in the Detweiler's living room and finished the remains of the food.

"They're very romantic," said Patricia. "Don't you have them?"

Josie shook her head.

"What route are they taking this year?" Patricia asked.

"Around Granger's Wood and across towards the reservoir," Sally answered, making Nick think she was on the committee that organized it.

"Granger's Wood," one girl said in a low voice and gave a shudder.

"What's Granger's Wood?" Josie asked.

"It's supposed to be haunted," Sally said dismissively.

"The old Post Road ran through what's now Granger's Wood," Nick explained. "It was a main route from Boston to Hartford in pre-Revolutionary days. Towards the end of the Revolution, the road was re-routed to its present, er, route."

"It's funny," John said, picking up the story. "There seems to be no reason for it. If you look at the map, you can see that the road, which is generally straight, makes a sudden diversion, as if it were going around

14

something."

"Yeah, ghosts," Bill Patterson said.

"Naw," said Laura Mason, whose father was in real estate. "The land just got boggy there and they went around it. The stream is still there, and now it's just down from the reservoir. No mystery."

"Well, you believe what you want to," Nick said. "I don't think I believe in ghosts, but for a bit there, it's not a nice place."

"Is that the place with the ghost from the Revolution?" someone asked.

"What do you think?" Josie asked Patricia.

Patricia thought for a moment.

"I think I agree with Nick," she said softly, obviously not wishing to think about it too much.

The group was silent for a moment until Josie spoke.

"So what happens on a hay ride?"

"Oh, they're fun," Patricia said, happy to change the subject. "We all meet up and get in the back of open wagons full of hay – sometimes there's a line of them. It's loose hay, and there are some bales to lean against. You huddle up close in the cold night air as the wagon meanders down country roads. You end up in a barn for food and hot drinks and cider."

"You do that every year?" Josie asked.

Patricia looked down for a moment.

"It happens every year," she said. "I didn't go last

year, but the year before, it was good," she added brightly.

Patricia had found herself without a date the previous year. After Homecoming, she had stopped seeing Tom for reasons no one knew, and didn't go on the hayride, or to the Holly Ball. Even her Prom date was not what would have been expected. Supposedly she had been let down a week before the dance and had to endure the indignity of an "import" escort, essentially a blind date. Although both were stoically determined to have a good time, they had nothing in common.

The boys who knew her were sympathetic but the girls were enjoying a curious satisfaction in her perceived humiliation, and only grudgingly let their partners have a dance with her.

While Josie and Patricia were having their conversation, Sally maneuvered John and Nick away from them and towards the other end of the room.

"'What happens on a hayride?'" Sally mimicked. "Can you believe it? I mean, okay, they might not have hayrides in Rusty Horseshoe, Arizona, but you'd think she would have read about them!"

John laughed, but said, "Hayrides aren't written about much anymore. It's different here."

Sally's eyes flashed.

"No it's not different here. It's different *there* – out

where the tumbleweed rolls, and the rattlesnake bites, and the scorpion stings and the cactus pricks. I'm so sick of hearing about it! It's all I can do to get her to wear a skirt. Hell, she'll be in her element lying in the dusty hay being dragged in the dark by an arthritic nag."

Both Nick and John laughed at Sally's invective.

"It's not that bad," said Nick.

"You don't have to live with it," Sally moaned. "She complains because we don't have half the food she's used to. Endless Mexican, or grits or something that lives in a tree, down a hole, or under a rock."

"I think she'll fit in very well," John said. "It can't be easy being dropped into a group that's known each other since they were four years old."

Sally shrugged.

"Josie is odd," she said, lowering her voice. "The other day at school, someone mis-hit a tennis ball and it went on the roof of the library. There must be a hundred balls up there. Josie leaves the court – she didn't even hit it – it was that stupid Jane Finch – and goes to the corner of the library and climbs up the wall to the roof. She threw down a dozen balls, then climbed down and continued the game."

"Excellent!"

"No, Nick, you just don't do that at Pinehill," she explained patiently. "I was mortified!"

"Why?"

"Oh, don't be deliberately obtuse!" she exclaimed. "Oh, there's Tommy Bradford."

She left just as Patricia and Josie rejoined them.

"Patricia's been telling me about all the events for the rest of the year," Josie said. "It all sounds great fun, but I do miss the big barbecues and rodeos."

She went quiet for a moment.

"Missing your horse?" John said facetiously, but Josie's eyes welled up and he instantly apologized.

"Oh, Josie! I'm sorry. I didn't know. Really!"

Josie sniffed and ignored two big tears that trickled down her cheeks.

"John's right," said Nick. "We really didn't know."

Patricia put her arm on Josie's.

"Come with me. We'll fix your make-up," she said.

"Nice one," said Nick when they had left.

John shrugged.

"Everyone's a jerk once in a while," he said.

Sally returned with Tom Bradford.

Nick cast a glance at John, who shook his head almost imperceptibly.

Tom was at the Academy, too, and Nick and John had known him almost as long as they had known each other. They found small doses of Tom enough and neither of them ever understood his popularity with girls.

"I see someone finally put Miss Arizona in her

place," Sally said. "Patricia's too nice to everyone. It doesn't get her anywhere. You'd think she'd have learned that after the disaster of the prom last year."

"It was my fault," said John.

"Oh, don't apologize. It's been a long time coming. I just said to Tommy that it was time someone told her what's what. How did you do it? Say something nasty about her horse?"

Sally laughed loudly at her joke.

"Let's get some food," said Tom, and they went into the next room.

"It's not that much of a cultural shock coming to the East Coast, is it?" John asked.

"I wouldn't have thought so. Not nowadays," Nick replied. "Sally seems to think so, though."

"She's not going to do a return visit, is she?" John said, then laughed heartily.

"I can't see her shaking scorpions out of her stilettos," Nick agreed and laughed.

"I *can* see her pounding a snake with one, though," John said and they laughed again.

"Good party, isn't it?" Tom said coming back to them as they continued to laughed.

"Detweiler parties are always good," said Nick.

"I don't know how many more of them there can be," said Tom. "What with the way things are."

John started to ask what he meant, but Nick spoke

first. "You met Sally's cousin, didn't you, Tom?"

"Calamity Jane? Yeah, Sally introduced us earlier. Why?"

"She's very nice. I thought you might have liked her."

Tom looked wary. He came from another old family, but one, perhaps a little too restricted in its breeding habits.

"Er, yes," he stammered. "Seemed very pleasant, but Sally – "

"We thought you might be taking her to the hayride," Nick said.

Tom was nonplussed.

"I think Sally was expecting – "

"Sorry," said John. "You've got a date already."

Tom considered this.

"Never mind, Tom," said Nick.

"We were just making sure the way was clear. Didn't want to step on anyone's toes," John said. "Thirty thousand acres. Quite athletic, too."

"I'm going with Sally," Tom finally blurted out. "We agreed last week."

"Ah, well," said John. "That's fine. We'll see you there."

"Sally's such a good old friend, we didn't want to see her left out," Nick said. "One has to be fair to old friends, and she and John did have a vague understanding. Hard luck, John."

John looked at the floor, aware of Tom's growing discomfiture.

"I think I'll ask Sally why she broke our agreement," John said eventually.

Tom lurched towards him, but Nick cut him off.

"I'd fix things with Josie first," he said. "Someone might beat you to it."

John nodded.

"Good point. See you later, and thanks, Tom."

Tom looked bewildered, but went to talk to Sally.

"Oh, hell," said John. "I guess I'll have to ask Josie now."

"I'll see you later, then," Nick said. "I've got to get a date for myself."

ॐ

The night was clear and the moon nearly full. The horses clopped slowly down the lane with about thirty couples sprawled in the back of three wagons.

Josie, completely at home behind a horse, lay back against John and watched the clouds move over the moon.

"The nights are different here," she said. "During the day things are pretty much the same as in Arizona, but they look different – if you know what I mean. But, at night, it's *completely* different."

John gently tightened his arm around her to show he was listening.

"Do you know what I mean?" she asked, sitting up and looking at him.

Across the wagon, Sally rolled her eyes, and only half turning to Tom said loudly, "She's at it again. She has the most – "

"Tell us more," Patricia said.

Sally made a bored face and lay her head back on Tom's chest, but Tom inclined his head towards Josie.

"Yes, go on, Josie," he said.

If it seemed to surprise Josie that her remark had attracted an audience, she wasn't intimidated.

Josie laughed easily.

"I wasn't meaning anything profound," she said. "I just think that night times in places you don't know are very different. I'm not particularly scared of things. I mean, I grew up with poisonous snakes, scorpions and birds that swoop down and grab animals in front of you.

"But lanes like this are foreign to me," she continued. "The stone fences – as you call them – and the bare trees are part of a darkness that's unfamiliar. Not frightening, really, but a darkness that's full of things I don't know and can only imagine."

"Yes!" exclaimed Patricia. "I understand. We grew up here and know the woods and fields, and even make up stories about them – "

"As if to make them mysterious," Tom put in, "because we know they're not."

"Mmm," said Patricia, nodding agreement.

"So what stories have been made up?" Sally asked with a sneer. "I don't recall any. It's not like there's anything like Spooner's Well or Spider Gates around here."

Tom looked at her with a disapproval that could be seen in the moonlight. We could also see that Josie's eyes were wide.

"Spider Gates?" she asked.

"Just a spooky story boys tell to get girls to hang on to them," Sally said. "There aren't any creepy stories about here. It's *too boring!*"

Tom glared at her to be quiet, so she sulked.

The sound of the horses and the low murmur of the other couples in the wagon echoed louder as they approached a low part of the lane and the temperature dropped as they grew nearer the stream.

The sound of water gently moving over stones mingled with the hoof-beats.

"Did you just feel it get colder?" Nick asked.

"One story that was supposed to happen around here was about a Red Coat who got lost," Nick began, and all but Sally looked towards him. "He had been part of the contingent in Boston that had moved westwards after Lexington and Concord. A number traveled to New York via Springfield and Hartford instead of going through Providence.

"Some locals a few miles from here thought it would be good to pick off the company as they came through. In a day of sniping and running skirmishes, they took the company down to about a dozen, until those remaining either surrendered or took off their red coats and headed for the woods.

"They eventually found all the bodies – except one who is still occasionally seen, trying to find his way out of these woods and back to Boston and England."

There was an appreciative silence when he finished.

"I never – " Sally began.

"Good story, Nick," Tom interrupted.

"Is it true?" Patricia asked.

"Who knows?" Nick said. "People say they hear or see him along this road at night."

"Give me a break!" Sally exclaimed.

"It's believable," Patricia replied, ignoring her. "It's really dark, too."

"Does it matter if it's true? It's a good story," said Josie. "I don't think good stories should be challenged too much."

"Even if they're nonsense?" Sally asked.

Josie didn't reply at once.

"Nonsense is good once in a while."

The couples whispered together quietly, except for Tom and Sally. Tom gazed resignedly at the stars while Sally continued to sulk.

The wagon slowed a little as it began moving up hill after crossing the stream, and the slower pace made it seem much more quiet.

Curiously, it was Sally who seemed most aware of this and she stiffened and looked at the others, nestled comfortably in the hay.

They were all nodding in a quiet daze. Tom almost seemed to be asleep. As she looked again at her companions, she saw they were talking and moving normally. Tom looked from the stars to her.

"Are you all right?" he asked.

"I used to think so," she said.

He put his arm around her shoulder and gently drew her towards him, but she remained tense.

It seemed to her that she was the only one who was fully awake; who had all her senses working, and who heard the thrashing in the undergrowth at the side of the road and saw a face appear momentarily through the bushes, illuminated by the moon, and then disappearing just as suddenly.

Instantly stiffening, Sally sat up straight and opened her mouth to scream, but nothing came out. In the instant that it would have taken to recover her voice, she questioned whether she had really seen anything.

Of course, she had; but why had no one else?

She looked about her. The horses clopped on obliviously and equally the driver remained huddled in his great coat and muffler, with a blanket across his lap and legs.

The other couples talked softly, or kissed, or just looked dreamily about at nothing in particular, while she, Sally Hawes, was about as detached from her date as she could get.

She looked at Tom to find him staring at her.

"What's the matter?" she asked him more sharply than she intended.

"Just looking at you and wondering why you're so unhappy," he answered softly. "I haven't upset you, have I?"

"Did you see – ?" she started to ask, but stopped. "I don't know, Tom. It's not you. I've been edgy since Josie arrived. I've lost my privacy at home and I have to share my friends everywhere else."

Tom smiled.

"Friends are for sharing; you get more that way," he said.

"Well, I only have to share them for one more week," she answered. Sally looked at Tom's earnest face and smiled in spite of herself. "I'm sorry, I've been a bitch. You don't deserve this."

"No, I don't," he said.

She moved to him and rested her head on his shoulder and closed her eyes.

The image of the face appeared in her memory. It

was clear, real and she knew, unforgettable. Blue white in the moonlight with wide, almost wild, eyes and a gaping mouth.

The wagons drew up in front of the large wooden barn about twenty minutes later and the food crew – classmates without dates, or with allergies to hay or horses – greeted them with pottery mugs of cider.

Outside, the charcoal smoke swirled in the crisp air, mixed with the smells of hot dogs, hamburgers and corn on the cob.

Inside, the barn was subtly lit and the odd jack-o'lantern grinned down from a beam or ledge.

"This is great!" said Patricia loudly to the barn crew. She looked all around and enthused at the hanging apples, the scarecrows wearing bits of school uniform and holding pennants of local schools.

Nick caught up with her and she took his arm easily as they went out to get some food.

"Now all this needs is some good old country music," exclaimed Josie, looking around the barn again.

Several people laughed casually, both at the suggestion and the way she said it.

"Well, why not? It's fun. And it fits in a barn!" she said. "Don't you think it's a good idea?" Sally watched John closely to see how he'd answer.

"It's the right setting," he agreed, "but country music for some reason isn't all that popular in this part of the country."

"Really? I can't think why not," she exclaimed. "Perhaps it's just too lively." "You may be right," said John, and led her to the food table.

"We're not fans of *The Beverley Hillbillies* either," Sally said, not quite *sotto voce*.

"Have you ever heard such nonsense?" Sally exclaimed to Tom, Nick and Patricia, almost before Josie was out of ear-shot.

"It's natural, enough," Patricia said.

Sally snorted.

"Why can't you enjoy yourself?" Tom asked, finally exasperated.

"Enjoy myself?! With *her* around? Everyone thinks she's *cute* or *quaint* or *different* when she's nothing. Do you know she can hardly keep up at school? Hasn't read *any* Dickens or Salinger, or Henry James.

"She can add and subtract, but her accent in French is unbelievable."

"But isn't she fluent in Spanish?" Nick asked.

"Hrmph! Spanish. Who speaks Spanish?"

"Most of the world," Patricia answered softly.

"Has beens. Lost empires. Lost chances, like you," she spat.

Patricia flinched but didn't falter.

"I'm not sure what you mean, Sally," she said firmly. "And I'm not sure why you're cross with me."

"Because I'm fed up with losers!" Sally shouted, no longer caring. "You're all losers; doomed to spend whatever's left of your family's money and never account for anything yourselves. The best any of you can hope for is to marry into money, but it will be to people with names like Kralevski, or Tshersarwitz, or Goney, not anyone of – of – *style!*"

"Sally," Tom began.

"You're the same, Tom," Sally said sharply. "You're just as doomed."

"We're not doomed, Sally," said Nick, moving forward. "Has she been drinking?" he asked Tom quietly.

"No, I haven't been drinking," Sally shouted. "I've been *thinking* – clearly for a change."

She separated herself from them, but they still tried to protect her from all the others and keep the scene relatively private.

"Someone has to be drunk to talk like this, do they?" she asked loudly.

Patricia moved forward.

"Sally, come talk to me," she said gently. "You can't argue with all of them."

"Can't I?" she asked defiantly. "No, you're right. I can't, because you're all disappearing like the Wicked Witch of the West. Losing your positions, your jobs, your money. In twenty years, none of you will be here; none of our families will be running anything and the world will be run by people from Tucson, or Dubuque, or Boise – not Boston, New York or Philadelphia!"

Josie had listened quietly until this outburst. Now, with her eyes filled with tears – rage and mortification, she turned to John.

"Take me home, please."

"Sure."

John gently put his arm around Josie, turned to the others and murmured goodnights and walked down the lane to where the cars were parked.

Nick led Patricia away to another corner of the barn. Patricia had tears running down her cheeks, but though profoundly shocked, was calm.

"Why does she hate me? I thought we were friends. I've known her all my life," she repeated in utter confusion.

Back in the barn, Tom faced Sally. She alone stood defiant, angry, and still very pretty.

"One day I hope you'll tell me what this was all about," he said.

CR

By Thursday the following week, the boys had thought about that evening's events but hadn't spoken about it much.

Nick and Tom stood in front of Dexter's waiting for the bus. Snow was falling and they could feel the temperature dropping.

"Is Patricia okay?" Tom asked.

"She didn't know what hit her," Nick said. "I called her the next day. She didn't want to talk about it, but she invited me to the Holly Ball."

"That's great! It will give her something to think about," Tom said. "Sally asked me while we were in the hay wagon, but if she thinks I'm going with her after that psychotic outburst, she's got another thing coming! She's going to have to do more than make prissy apologies, too."

"Have you told her you're not going yet?" Nick asked.

"No. I'm saving that for the weekend."

Two boys moved towards them. Stu had his leg in plaster and was awkwardly wielding his crutches while Buzz carried his book bag.

"You never did tell us what happened to you," Nick said.

The boy with the victim laughed.

"Were you there, Buzz?"

"Yes, I was there," he conceded.

Stu Gardner leaned against the building and disentangled himself from the arm clasps of the crutches and Buzz Keogh put the book bags down.

"Okay," Stu began. "I'll tell you, if you tell us what went on with Sally Hawes at the hayride."

Tom gave a loud "Humph!" and shook his head. "I

wish I knew. She was nuts all evening. Okay, Sally was always a little highly strung, but she was fun and funny. But on Saturday, oh man, she was somewhere else!"

"So we heard," said Stu.

"Well, her cousin Josie had driven her partially nuts – stealing her friends and center-stage; but how that turned into the attack on poor Patricia Detweiler and the rest of us – well, it beats me."

Nick nodded.

"She never settled that evening. She was nervous all the way in the wagon," Tom said. "I thought we'd get some making out going, but it was like she was on lookout duty."

"I think something spooked her," Nick said, and Tom agreed.

"Er, how?" Stu asked.

"I don't know. There were some stories, then Nick told the Red Coat story," Tom said. "But she was pretty edgy before then."

"Ah, the old Red Coat story," Buzz said. "The one that's supposed to haunt the woods by Oakdale?"

"Yeah," Nick said, "but the story gets applied to any woods in the state. I first heard it about Granger's Wood and told it that way. I don't suppose anyone knows which woods it really is."

"Didn't Sally know the story?"

"I guess not," said Tom.

Sally and Josie came round the corner together and went into Dexter's without speaking to us.

"I'm out of here," Tom said, picking up his books and heading down the street.

A moment later, Josie came out of the store and went up to Nick, Buzz and Stu in her usual open way.

"Hi," she said. "Been waiting long?"

"Few minutes."

"Doesn't Sally want to talk to us?" Nick asked.

"Yes," Josie said, "but not with me here. Still she'll be able to have you all to herself next week. I'm flying home Saturday."

There were murmurs of "We'll miss you," and "Have a good flight," or, "Where has the time gone?"

"I've just stopped to say good-bye," she said. "I'm the one that has some shopping to do. My friends back home won't believe what girls here wear unless I take some things for them to see."

"Are you going to get that slinky dress?" Nick asked, nodding towards the window.

Josie laughed.

"No, but you should see the one that Sally just put a big deposit on for the Holly Ball," she said before turning to Buzz and Stu.

"Bye, Buzz, Stu," she said kissing, their cheeks lightly. "Bye, Nick," she said, shaking his hand. "I'll tell my friends all about you guys. Don't forget me. You can even write."

She waved and went back into the store.

"She was nice," Stu said.

"Different, but nice," Buzz said in agreement.

They were laughing when Sally came out of Dexter's carrying her school bag.

"Hi, Sally," they said.

"Life's going back to normal, we hear," Buzz said.

"I can't wait," Sally said heavily. "What a shock to the system she was! Thanks for being nice to her," Sally said. "I couldn't cope, as you saw. I'm sorry. I'm going to have to spend the next months apologizing and try to make up to you and Tom, and to poor Patricia.

"Oh! I don't mean poor poor – though she is, or will be soon. She needs to learn something that will support her as the boys won't buzz around her without the fortune. I suppose she could be cute if she did something with her hair and smartened up her wardrobe. She's got a good figure under there somewhere, I think."

"It's a shame Josie will miss the Holly Ball," Stu said, trying to imagine Josie in an elegant dress. "She would have enjoyed that."

"I wouldn't have," Sally said. "She would have turned it into a barn dance. Anyway, at least I've got a date for that. I've been looking at dresses. They've put one aside I can pick up tomorrow. Tom will just love it!"

Sally looked at Stu.

"What happened to you? Is it broken?"

"Last Saturday night. We were setting up at the barn when Brainy Buzz here had the bright idea of trying to find the hay wagons by running through the woods parallel to the road, trying to startle people, and then hitch a lift back to the barn."

Nick laughed his approval of the scheme, but Sally had gone pale.

"It went well enough until I fell down a hole," Stu said. "Just when we were about to break out of the woods onto the road."

"We would have surprised everyone," Buzz said, "but dickhead here thought he saw something and was so startled that he disappeared down a rabbit hole and I had to walk two miles to get my car and take him to the hospital. Missed all the fun."

"Never mind," said Sally. "There's always next year."

Thoughts and Whispers

Old School Tie

Thoughts and Whispers

Old School Tie

One's first teaching job is fraught with terror under the best of circumstances. I hardly knew what to expect the first time I faced a class of boys, nor had the faintest idea how I would fill up those long weeks, each with thirty-four lessons.

For some reason there was a shortage of teachers the year I applied for my post. I had just taken my degree and was unwilling to completely sever the cord which bound me to Cantab. I thought I could stretch it to a school in the fens, or perhaps even as far as the Broads, but I had no wish to leave East Anglia.

I found the advertisement for Crockfield Hall rather by accident. Apparently it had fallen from another student's notebook, for it was a mimeographed sheet with the details of three jobs on it: one for English, one for maths and one for history.

In due course, I applied, was granted an interview and was offered the post. The school I visited on the day of the interview in late May seemed much different from the one I carried my bags to in early September. Subtle changes of atmosphere, coupled with my own feelings of uneasiness, gave Crockfield Hall a particularly cold, desolate and forsaken feeling. But, as the Second

Master pointed out, the boys hadn't yet arrived and all schools feel unnatural without them. The Second Master seemed affable at the interview, but now he was a little eccentric and made me feel uncomfortable.

He showed me my room, helped me with my bags, told me where things were, then left.

My room was in an attic garret, just off a first year dormitory. The Headmaster had said at the interview that there wasn't much I could do wrong with first years. I would look after thirty and be master and slave to them.

I put my books in my small bookcase, hung up my clothes; my academic gown – too new, too stiff, too black. The room had one window of leaky leaded glass which looked over a vast expanse of roof tiles and chimneys. The room was at the corner of the large rectangular building. The main building had a large central hall with a high domed ceiling. My room looked out partially on the glass dome and partially over the slope and chimneys of the South Wing.

Later that month, I would be able to tell precisely which direction the wind came from by the pitch of the eerie notes caused by the chimneys, turrets and curiously arranged roof angles. Indeed, on some nights, the wind tore round my corner so powerfully that I was afraid that the window would be sucked out.

I was essentially alone in the school for three days

before the boys returned. I found my way around, learnt room numbers, and ensured that I would not crash into the Headmaster's study while in search of the Common Room. Even with three days to let my imagination work, the school took on no particular atmosphere. It was simply an old building, badly lighted, badly heated, badly insulated and ineffectually maintained. Like most schools.

When the boys arrived, there was no time to think. I had to see them unpacked and sorted out. I showed them round the school and explained the rules. I made sure that they were properly turned out and lined up for dinner.

The Hall was large and bleak. It was mock-Gothic and ill-proportioned. Sounds rumbled round it and even conversation with your neighbour took on the hollow garble thought unique to London railway termini.

I met the other new masters. Macaulay was the History man. Crockfield was his second school and it wasn't nearly as good as the one he left.

"They seem to do everything backwards here. The timetable's a shambles. Only five history periods a week in form four and just two hours' prep."

The Maths master, though 'new' was ancient and sullen. He had come from a boys' school which had decided to admit girls. He had been at the school for eighteen years and suffered numerous indignities but refused to tolerate this latest outrage. It seemed that he had yet to speak to anyone. Even I, in my inexperience, realised it would be an impertinence to speak to him this term.

Prefects looked after the boys after dinner and the masters joined in the Common Room for coffee. A fire was burning brightly and the room was cosy and filling up nicely with pipe smoke. There was animated conversation among the old staff members, but Macaulay and I stood uneasily in a corner, afraid to squat in some senior's chair.

After a while, Dr Mackle, my department head, approached.

"Settling in all right?" he asked.

"Dreading tomorrow," I said.

"Don't worry, we all do. Anyway, tomorrow's easy. It's the next hundred seventy-nine days that are the buggers." He shook his head sorrowfully. "If you'd like to sit down, you can use that chair."

He pointed to one in the far corner.

"I don't suppose anyone would mind. It was Harrison's chair, but. . . ."

"Thank you."

I took my coffee and crossed the room.

New staff are paradoxical. Everyone notices them, but no one pays attention to them. If one is quiet and respectful, they ignore and despise. If you are opinionated and voluble, they tend to think you'll be one of them in five years, but they still ignore you. New members of staff who stick together are accused of being anti-social. But after a number of years, the cliques are just the same, but accepted by everyone, except the newest members of staff.

At eight o'clock, without having had a single intelligent conversation with any of the three Oxbridge graduates, I excused myself and went to check the first years.

The prefects had got them to bed and switched off the lights. The dorm was lit only by the glow from the prefects' area behind a makeshift partition in the corner. The two prefects in my dorm were Matthews and Greene. They were rather weedy lads, which is probably why they were assigned to a form one dormitory.

I tapped on their partition before sticking my head in.

"Go to bed and shut up, you feeble wart!" one of them shouted.

I put my head in.

They leapt to their feet, scattering playing cards on the floor.

"Sorry, sir. We thought you were one of the lower forms of life, sir."

"No doubt. All quiet on the western front?"

"Sir?"

"Any trouble?"

"No, sir."

"Good night, then."

"Good night, sir," answered Rosencrantz and Guildenstern.

Then, when I had left, in whispered tones:

"Western front?"

"He's an English master, you silly sod."

"Oh."

My room was cold and felt damp. By my single light, I read for a while and then decided to sleep. It was nine fifteen. The dorm was quiet except for the sound of a child whimpering quietly.

∝

It rained the next day. The confusion and the curious turn of events which followed are covered with a layer of mud in memory.

Boys were roused at six-thirty and turned out for the morning run round the playing fields. Fresh white kits and bright new plimsols came back sodden and mud-encrusted. A hurried push through the showers and then into uniform. I managed to get them to breakfast only five minutes late.

Breakfast was a surprisingly pleasant affair. I had expected Dotheboys Hall fare of runny, lukewarm gruel and undrinkable tea. At the masters' table, there was animated discussion and good humour. I took courage and looked forward to getting started.

Chapel service came and went with the predictable hymns and cliché-ridden, but grand sounding, promises for the term, the year, and, indeed, the rest of our lives.

The first day, I managed to hand out the necessary books and sort through the register of all the boys. I found all the classrooms at the right periods and managed to keep five seconds ahead of them all day. Except for one second form period.

The boys had filed in and stood behind their desks. I told them to be seated and did a rapid head count. Twenty-three.

Since I had twenty-two names on my list, I called the roll. Everyone answered. I then asked for the name of the boy whose name I had not called.

There was no reply.

I counted heads again and made it twenty-three.

"There is some sleepy boy here whose name I didn't read out and who has not identified himself."

I ignored a giggle.

Still, there was no response.

"All right," I said, determined to catch them out.

"Everyone stand up. Now, when I call your name, sit down."

I watched them carefully.

"Atherton, Brockley, Campbell, ffollett. . . ."

I looked up frequently to ensure two didn't sit down at once.

"White, Williams, Young."

I came to the end of the list and no one was standing. In desperation, I asked if there were two boys of the same surname, fully aware that they were expecting me to start braying at any moment.

No response. I counted heads again. There were twenty-two boys. I counted yet again. Twenty-two.

I was puzzled and proud, but I refused to waste any more time. I carefully counted out twenty-two exercise books and handed them out. Twenty-two.

Other classes went well enough, but I continued to be perplexed by the discrepancy in the second form.

I spent time after dinner in my study talking to individual first year boys and ensuring that they were not too frightened or miserable, but I kept strictly formal and showed as little sympathy as possible.

My room was very cold and I resolved to ask the bursar if the fireplace could be reopened as my electric fire was feeble and only emphasised the cold in the rest of the room.

I had no marking to do as yet and had managed to organise the next day's lessons during study hall. I decided to write some letters. However, after twenty minutes, I gave up because my hands were too cold. I decided to look for some place warmer.

The Common Room was empty and the fire nearly out, so I abandoned the idea of working there. But coming across the Central Hall, I saw a light shining from beneath the library door.

The library was very large for a school of Crockfield's size. It contained nearly twenty thousand volumes and was laid out like a literary man's dream: bookshelves along all four walls from floor to ceiling with a gallery running right round the room and spiral staircases in the corners.

A vast oriental rug covered the floor and there were large tables with low green-shaded lamps and large well-worn, soft leather arm chairs scattered about next to smaller tables and standard lamps.

"Good evening, James," I said to Dr Mackle.

"Oh. Hello. Get too cold for you up there?"

Dr Mackle was seated in one of the leather chairs, smoking his pipe. The room was redolent of Balkan Sobranie. There was a glass of port on his table, and a folio of something on his lap.

"Glass of port?" he asked.

"Thank you."

"Behind the librarians' desk on the right."

I looked. An antique tantalus was on the shelf and half a dozen glasses.

"It's not locked. I must get you a key for that. One of the few perks."

I looked at the decanters.

"Port, brandy and Madeira. We're given two bottles

a week of each. The bursar reckons it's cheaper than heating oil. You might as well drink it. We only get two bottles if more than one and a half is drunk. We can't accumulate it. Good system, really."

I poured myself a brandy and took it to the chair beside his table.

"Settling in all right?"

"I suppose it's really too early to tell. No problems, though. Except my room is bloody cold. I dread to think what it will be like in winter. I'm going to ask the bursar if the fireplace can be opened up. I wouldn't mind buying my own wood or coal."

"Use old prep books. There are also cupboards full of old exam papers. No one will miss them."

The library was warm because it was over the furnace and ancient iron grills were dotted along the edge of the room.

"Warmest place in the school, this," Mackle said.

"Why aren't there more people here?"

"Boys get thrown out at nine, and not all master's rooms are as cold as yours. As a matter of fact, that's why I'm here. I used to have your study when I first came. I got into the habit of coming here each evening and never got out of it. There is the port, too. Of course, you'll find that as the work comes in, there will be more in here. Can't talk then, though."

"How long have you been here?"

"At Crockfield? Twenty-three years. I had one job for a few years at the Perse, but decided I must get away from Cambridge. Frightful syndrome, the Oxbridge habit. It scars one for life."

We chatted for a while longer, mostly about the English syllabus, but then he read and I wrote until eleven.

I went through the dormitory and checked that all was in order. The prefects were asleep and all was silent until I was in my room and then the faintest sound of a child whimpering penetrated the cold and the dark.

Feeling concern for the wretched boy, I opened my door and went into the dormitory. Whoever it was didn't want to be found out, for all was quiet.

When I was in bed, however, the sobbing resumed and continued until I fell asleep.

I saw the bursar at breakfast the following morning and asked about the fireplace.

"I'd have no objection to paying for the coal or the chimney sweep if you needed to get one."

"No, no. We can have that done by our own maintenance people. We'll see how much coal you use before talking about charging you."

"How did the other masters survive that room so long?" I asked.

"Less sensitive, I suppose. Several had paraffin heaters and at one stage they were going to put gas fires in the rooms. And there were those who only slept there and lived in the Common Room or the library."

"Perhaps I'm being unreasonable – "

"Not at all. We won't get to it for a few days."

"No rush, Before winter, though, please."

"Right you are."

The bursar made a note in his diary, then dripped coffee on it.

It *is* the second, third and fourth day that try the new teacher. The boys weren't difficult, merely crafty. They tested how much whispering they could get away with; if I'd notice they'd changed places; how I'd react to a Perspex ruler being reflected in my eyes; what I'd do if they were late, and so on.

Whether I passed these little tests, I would find out in a few weeks' time. One thing I felt confident of was my own organization. Twelve weeks of purgatory in teaching practice had taught me to always have three extra lessons up my sleeve for any given period. Children, rightly so, show an active resentment of incompetence. Only when they are adult do they recognise mediocrity as an acceptable standard.

I realised the simple tactic of appearing busy before the boys was an effective one. I took a large stack of marking into the study hall and showed profound irritation at any disturbance. It became clear that I wouldn't prowl around looking for trouble if they let me get on with my work.

After study hall, I asked to see Ros and Guil to see if they knew who the whimperer was.

They shook their heads.

"I'm afraid we're both sound sleepers," said one of them.

"Does no one appear to be particularly miserable?"

"No, sir. They all seem to be equally so."

"Who is the youngest boy here?" I asked.

"Daniels, sir," they both said.

"He's adjusting all right?"

"Yes, sir. He fairly loves it. He hates his home, but he doesn't live with his parents."

"Oh?"

"You see, sir, his parents were divorced again and custody was given to his step-father, who has since remarried."

"Extraordinary."

"He doesn't like it much, so he thinks this place is wizard, sir."

"Wizard? Is that word back in use?"

"You mean it isn't new?"

"Hardly."

"Well, it's new to Crockfield. Don't spoil it for them."

"I wouldn't dream of it."

"Is that all, sir."

"Yes. Keep your ears open, though. There's a very

unhappy boy here."

"Right-ho, sir."

Both prefects would be profoundly saddened when they learnt that Bertie Wooster had been dead for decades.

In the evening, after coffee in the Common Room, I took my marking into the library. I was the only one there, but presently Macaulay arrived.

"Keeping afloat?" he asked.

"So far, so good."

"I feel I've told them everything I know already. I came in here to mug up some new history."

"You're joking."

"I only got a third, remember."

"Shh. Walls have ears. Want a brandy?"

"Love one. Not much chance. You got a bottle in your study?"

I showed him the tantalus.

"My, my! The old place isn't so bad after all. How's your room?"

"Freezing."

"Typical. Mine's an oven and the windows are painted shut. Any trouble in your dorm?" he asked.

"No. My prefects need wringing out and hanging in the airing cupboard, and there's a boy who cries late at night, but I don't know who."

"Ah! You've got the Crockfield Whimperer."

I laughed.

"Is that what he's called. Who is he?"

"No, no, old boy. He doesn't exist. It's one of the Crockfield ghosts. Some poor lad who was miserable here years ago and wandered into the fens. Never did find him. Must have been an awful stink. Anyway, he whimpers about the place from time to time. Tell him to shut up and hang garlic on your door."

Other staff came into the library and we had to be quiet. I worked for two hours in the glorious warmth of the room and the muffled noises of study.

The following morning, the bursar told me that they'd start on my study that afternoon.

"Put anything you don't want covered in brick dust and soot under your bedclothes. They'll open it up today and de-coke the chimney tomorrow. I've found some fire irons and a scuttle. There's probably a grate still in there, but if not, there are dozens in the cellars. We'll have you warm by the weekend."

"Getting your fire, eh?" Dr Mackle asked across the table.

"Today. At least they're opening it up. Tomorrow I should have some warmth."

"Good, good. Though I shan't be seeing you in the library any more, then."

Before my first class, I went up to my room to clear my things from the area of the fireplace. Many things were still in piles, so I had to shift rather a lot. I had just gathered an armful of books when I heard the soft mournful sobbing again. This time it gave me a real start; partly because of what Macaulay had said, and partly because I had just come through the dormitory and it was empty.

I threw the books on the bed and ripped my door open and charged into the dorm.

There was no one there. I heard a creak and saw the door to the corridor and staircase drift shut. Bolting across the room, I flung it open, but no one was in the hallway or on the stairs.

With a sudden inspiration, I went to the prefects' room and looked in. It would not have been the first time that a new master had been fooled by a tape recording.

But their room was in order. I had a quick look under the tables and beds. I even checked the electrical points to see if there were wires leading to a time switch and a tape recorder.

The room was hopelessly bare. No doubt Ros and Guil were scientists. Aside from two photographs pinned to the inside of their wardrobes (anatomically and aesthetically pleasing) there wasn't a single bit of decoration in their room, let alone the electronic gadgetry necessary to drive a school master mad.

I was late for chapel. I grabbed my gown and tore

across the quad and sneaked in, hopefully unnoticed. The morning service consisted of a badly sung hymn, an irrelevant reading and a number of announcements which no one listened to. On better days, it would be a familiar reading, but why anyone would think Chronicles suitable for school assembly was beyond me. Still, the motions of tradition were there. The routine had been set by the founders two hundred years before and never altered. I remembered my own school days with the endless repetitions of the twenty-third psalm.

I later found that the headmaster of Crockfield read ten verses each day, and slowly worked his way through the Old and New Testaments. The only failure in this plan was due to his strict adherence to ten verses. He began and ended in curious places and often continuity of action was lost.

I had a word with the bursar after chapel and told him that the room was ready anytime the men wanted to begin.

The thought of having a warm room was too delicious to keep from my mind and throughout the day I imagined myself reading by a cosy fire. That thought affected my whole attitude and I was lenient and generous that morning.

At lunch time I had a quick look into my study to see if they had begun, but they had not. I felt embarrassed and reflected that it was like waiting for

Father Christmas.

I had the second form after lunch and gave a fair performance in a reading of Poe's "The Cask of Amontillado", and a lively discussion followed. I took heart that some literature could still capture the imagination and provoke genuine enthusiasm.

At the end of the lesson, for no reason that I was aware of, I once again counted the boys as they filed out of the room.

There were twenty-three.

That number chilled me to the bone. That prime number, that fatal number, uttered by Madame Defarge as the blade fell. That number of my years on earth.

I resented the upset. That number, probably yet another miscount, (after all, English masters aren't supposed to be good at maths) had banished my good humour so thoroughly that I snapped at my dedicated lower sixth when I entered the room.

In the middle of a totally unwarranted tirade about manners, one of the prefects knocked on the door.

"Excuse me, sir. The headmaster would like a word with you."

"Now?"

"He said to fetch you at once, sir."

I followed the prefect to the headmaster's study.

I don't know what I expected when I arrived, but I did not expect to find the headmaster flanked by the local constable and a detective inspector.

I confess to some relief at seeing them, for then I knew it was not I who was in trouble; for whatever I had done, it did not require summoning the police.

"Sit down," the headmaster said. "I'm afraid there is some rather distressing news. It only concerns you indirectly. By the way, have you seen Dr Mackle this morning?"

I hadn't.

The police were called because the cleaning of my chimney had dislodged the bones of a young boy. It was estimated he had been there for a generation. It was supposed that this was the boy who had been thought lost in the fens.

"I have to tell you," said the headmaster, "that at the time of the boy's disappearance, Dr Mackle was in charge of that dormitory, and that was his room."

"Was the boy known for whimpering?" I ventured.

The head nodded.

"Dr Mackle complained of it all the time," the head continued. "He said it was driving him mad."

ॐ

Never again did I hear the Crockfield Whimperer. Though on certain November nights, when the wind is from the northeast, straight off the North Sea and the fens, it causes a disconcerting whistling in the chimney.

Crockfield Hall managed to escape with a minimum

of bad publicity, but the police never did find Dr Mackle. Mackle was right about one thing, though – I never did see him in the library again. But very occasionally, I do catch a whiff of Balkan Sobranie.

Die Schöne Welt
A Westbury Tale

.

Thoughts and Whispers

Die Schöne Welt
A Westbury Tale

The name of Anthony Tripp (1896-1979) is known by everyone who has paid slight attention to fiction in the past thirty years. His books have been printed, reprinted, produced as plays, films and television shows. He was a novelist who had attracted some early fame, but was later disregarded by the critics.

Yet, he wrote so prolifically, and in a style which had instant appeal, that he remained in the public eye throughout his life. The publication of a new Tripp novel delighted booksellers and mildly irritated the critics. They may have been pot-boilers as novels, but they were well-written and entertaining. Somerset Maugham maintained that was all that should be required of a novel.

Tripp proved himself to be a remarkable man in many ways. The openness of his life; his willingness to submit to countless interviews, photographers, journalists and other invaders of privacy, seems to contradict certain extraordinary truths about him.

In spite of his accessibility, he was not a media-junkie, but a quiet, modest man.

Tripp lived only a few miles from me, just outside Westbury, Massachusetts. I had seen him many times while growing up. Parents and friends would say, "There's Anthony Tripp," and I would catch a glimpse of his tall, rather elegant figure, and not understand why we never spoke to him.

Nonetheless, Anthony Tripp was a friendly and superficially sociable man. He was a popular figure at functions, plays, concerts and even local high school football games. I say "superficially sociable" because while he appeared in public and mingled with many acquaintances, no one claimed to be a close friend.

At school we never read any of Tripp's books. It wasn't until I went to college that I had more than a vague idea of who he really was or what he did.

I read his first novel during my freshman year. It was called *The Lion's Roar* and was about life in post-World War II Britain.

During my years at college, I read about half a dozen more of his books. One particularly impressed me and I wrote to Tripp to tell him so. He answered my over-enthusiastic letter with a brief note thanking me for taking the time to read his books and to write to him. He mentioned the volume which he was then writing. I had hoped he would notice that my home address, which I had used, was very near him and that he might invite me round so he could autograph a volume for me.

However, he did not.

In time, I became a writer for a small periodical. It was the sort of magazine, popular at the time, for which half a dozen people wrote everything under a variety of aliases – "pseudonym" and *"nom-de-plume"* were too up-market terms for what we did. One weekend, the publisher gave a large cocktail party for the advertisers to which staff writers and other guests were invited.

Anthony Tripp was there and it was then that I met him for the first time.

Why he had come, I didn't know, and judging from his expression, neither did he. He was not one of the guests of honor – though no one was certain who that was either. Due to some misunderstanding, there were two people actively claiming to be.

Tripp was friendly and unassuming. He retained his English accent. When I mentioned that he had been kind enough to write to me, he replied that he had always enjoyed writing to students.

"They ask intelligent questions. Also, I like giving them a line that they can throw into their term papers which will annoy their professors. I generally answer all letters from readers. It's good public relations, not to mention, common courtesy. It keeps one humble. Someone might write, 'I hated your last book. You killed off my favorite character. You're a beast!' I write and try to explain my motives. It's the slushy praise I can't bear.

"The letters I really like are those in which someone writes about an early book, which I have long written off. It is enormously pleasing to know they are still finding favor."

He told me that some people write to him regularly. These he calls his "faceless friends."

I was gratified that he spoke with me as long as he did, but he seemed to be trying to avoid the publisher, and the two guests of honor.

After several more drinks, I had reached the point where politeness dissipated. I asked him if he would inscribe a book for me. He named a day and suggested we meet one morning for coffee.

It teemed with rain the day I carried my copy of *Man and Beast* to a roadside diner that did all-day breakfasts and sandwiches.

His welcome was friendly. He was dressed in his usual suit, white shirt and bow tie, in marked contrast to the scruffy students or truck drivers with their tartan shirts and baseball caps.

He took my copy of *Man and Beast*, and, while I read the menu, wrote something in it and placed it on the table beside him.

"Have you read all my books?" he asked.

"I hope not. I hope there will be more."

"Very nice, but don't flatter me. Over the years, the critics have hardened me. But you didn't answer my question. Have you read all the novels?

"I haven't been able to find a copy of *Leipzig Lady*. There, are a few I haven't read, but I've got them all, except that one."

"No, you wouldn't have. It's only been printed once. There were about ten thousand copies of it, but second novels aren't reprinted the way first novels are.

"Also," he added, "it wasn't much good. I expect my most devoted readers would like to read it, but not enough to warrant a reprinting. Would you like to read it?"

"Very much."

"I can't give you a copy. I haven't got one. I gave it to the college. If you're serious about reading it, I will drop a note to the librarian and ask that you have access to it. You'll probably have to read it there."

We drained several cups of coffee and roamed through two hundred years of British and American fiction. When he had finished making comments on several contemporary novelists, he stared at me.

"What about you?" he asked.

"Me?"

"Don't you ever want to write anything decent?" he asked.

I sat there uncomfortably.

"I know I was no sky-rocket for the critics. Well, I wrote what I was capable of writing. Can you say the same?"

He was right, of course.

"No, I can't."

"Security and complacency, isn't it? That damnable magazine and its regular pay check for your third best effort. Am I right?"

"Yes."

"Can't you afford to do nothing for a while? Quit the job and write what you know you can?"

"Not easily," I stammered.

"It's not *supposed* to be easy, damn it!" he said sharply, and one or two heads turned.

"I could do a few short stories.

"Bugger short stories! Never wrote one in my life. All novels. Twenty-five of them. Fifteen best sellers. Still, it's what I do. Some people make cars, others furniture. I make novels. Novels can change the world.

"Go on, now. Get out of here and come back when you've written something."

His manner was easier now; teasing, but a firm instruction nonetheless.

"Contact me when you've read *Leipzig Lady*," he said, handing me my copy of *Man and Beast*.

I was bewildered when I returned home. I really didn't want to quit my job, and being told that one's not working hard enough is not pleasant to hear, especially when it's true.

I read *Leipzig Lady*. The library was expecting me and had the book behind the desk. I spent several evenings reading it, and I enjoyed watching the students come and go. I also spent time there thinking about my own writing and what I might do. The result was a short story of about thirty pages. It wasn't a novel, but after a lot of tweaking, I was happy with it and began another.

I contacted Tripp again and we met at the same diner.

When he sat down, all he said was, "Give me your chapters."

"I'm afraid it's short stories."

He glared at me and took them without a word.

We sat there drinking coffee as he read. His face gave nothing away when he finished the first one and began the shorter second. I occupied myself with a jelly doughnut. Then a cruller.

When he finished, he said nothing and slipped them back into the envelope and passed it back to me.

"Not bad," he said. "But then, I don't know anything about short stories. Never wrote one. Do you keep a journal? You should do. I've kept them for forty-five years. They record nearly all of what I did; what I'd read; stories people told me; the odd joke. They are invaluable to a writer when he is looking for situations," he said. "They also help me remember. When I get stuck, I go to one of the journals and either find an idea, or think of one while I'm looking. Other writers when they get stuck just torture the heroine," he smiled. "Sometimes I do that, too."

I'd been told about keeping a journal since we were taught about writing stories as children. I'd never done it. I did keep my desk calendars and appointment books, as they recorded everything I did.

"So, did you read *Leipzig Lady*?" Tripp asked.

"Yes, I did, and I enjoyed it."

"You see, though, with the present government in eastern Germany, it would be foolish to reissue it now. I'd be hounded by every right-wing organization in the western hemisphere."

"What made you write about Germany?"

He was about to drink his coffee when the waitress refilled his cup.

"If you ever get into this writing game seriously, you will realize that you have little control over what you write about," he said with an amused chuckle. "We control the words and sometimes the structure, but not the subject."

"Would you never allow it to be reprinted?"

"I suppose I would if anyone wanted to do *The Complete Novels of Anthony Tripp*, I wouldn't begrudge them my *Lady,*" he said with an ironic smile. "On its own, it wouldn't be a worthwhile venture. It's not one of the best."

"Which do you think is your best novel?"

"Ah! You shall have to wait before I tell you that," he said.

When we finished coffee, I took my stories and went home. It was bewildering to say the least. By the time I reached my apartment, I had worked myself into a pretty good rage and was prepared to take some decisive action. I read my own stories and let my own ego convince me that they were damn good - or at least better than anything I had read in a long time. Stuff the old goat! I'll send them off.

I met Tripp by accident a week or so later. He was ingloriously buying laundry detergent in a supermarket. Giants, too, have feet with mud.

He was in a jovial mood though I thought he was looking his age. I suggested we meet again for coffee, or lunch.

We met and continued our conversations. Unless I had a story to show him, these meetings were fairly short. He didn't eat much and I always had the sense that either I was keeping him from something, or he didn't want to get too close. Eventually, I ventured to invite him to my apartment, and he accepted.

It proved to be the first of many occasions. He fell into the habit of coming for a drink once or twice a month, on a Sunday evening. I was usually alone, but one day my girlfriend, Evelyne, wanted to meet him and was at my apartment when he came.

I'd been reluctant to foist other people on him, but I needn't have worried. He was charming and easy company and Evelyne liked him very much. She had read one or two of his books and was able to engage him with her own perceptions and point of view.

"He was probably glad to see a new face," she said to me after he'd left. "You said he didn't have close friends."

We continued to meet, sometimes at the diner, sometimes at my apartment. Evelyne was often there, but not always.

One day, he failed to appear at the diner. I wasn't wholly surprised. While he had never missed one of our meetings, I knew him to still be busy.

"Shouldn't you call him?" Evelyne asked.

"I don't want to intrude. He's got a lot more in his life than meeting me for coffee."

But, Evelyne was adamant. He was an old man. Anything could have happened. I was supposed to be his friend.

We drove to his house which was only ten minutes away.

There was no answer when we rang the bell and knocked on the door. While I was waiting patiently on the doorstep, Evelyne went around the house, looking in windows. Then she called from the rear of the house.

"Come! Quickly!"

I ran to the back and found her standing on a wheel barrow, looking in the kitchen window.

"He's in there!"

I saw nothing at first, but in the doorway to the inner hall, an arm was visible on the floor. By the time I climbed down, Evelyn smashed a window in the door with the heavy nozzle on the garden hose. We went in, called for an ambulance and waited.

ॐ

Several days later in the hospital, he had recovered enough to receive visitors. I took Evelyne, for she had certainly saved his life.

He was weak, but cheerful and apologized profusely for missing our meeting.

We spoke to the doctor on the way out. They were trying to locate any next of kin. Anthony Tripp had only a few weeks to live.

I had never heard him mention any family and suggested they try his publisher.

I thought about Tripp all that night. His death would be a major event. Everyone who had ever read one of his books would feel a personal loss. To me, this was a friend who was dying and a great man as well.

I visited Tripp every day. He asked me to bring books and magazines. Two weeks after he had been admitted, I went to the hospital to find he had discharged himself. A nurse told me that he wanted to die at home.

"I guess writers have a lot to do before they die," she said. "He'll probably have a great fire going."

"What?"

"A fire. They always have one going in the movies. Toss in all their bad stories and old love letters. Must be strange deciding what one is to be remembered by."

The nurse wasn't too far wrong. I called at Tripp's. His usually tidy drawing room was cluttered with boxes, papers and stacks of notebooks.

"Have you ever wondered what people would make of you if you were to die tomorrow?" he asked. "Consider, drawer by drawer, what you possess. It doesn't matter with private people, their odd habits go no further than a gossiping neighbor. I'm not that great a man, but I know that every scrap of paper I leave will be bid for, sold, published or pawed by some graduate student."

He gave a wry smile.

"They didn't want me to leave the hospital for a few more days. I told them I couldn't afford it.

"Take that box over there and come outside. We're going to have a bonfire." The light was fading rapidly, so I have no idea what the reams of papers contained. Occasionally, I saw a chapter heading explode in the flames and curl into ash. There were other pages which looked like poetry. Whether the works were Tripp's or not, I couldn't say.

We burned for more than an hour. More than once, I wondered at what was being lost, but to me, this was helping a personal friend, not depriving the world of important knowledge. In spite of that, I was uneasy.

When the flames eventually died down, we went inside. There remained only two cartons of papers which had not been destroyed. He thanked me for my help and asked me to return the following day. When I did, the room was filled with more boxes of paper.

"It's amazing what one saves, isn't it? I had every letter I'd ever received since 1925. Many were lost or destroyed during the war. Sometimes things happen for the best," he said enigmatically.

"These boxes aren't for burning," he said, indicating the array. Each box was dated to a five-year period. "I've left these to the college. If they don't want them, they can sell them, or burn them. Everything has now been edited. There is nothing here that I don't wish to be read after my death."

"Great secrets about to burst forth?" I teased.

"A few," he said quietly.

From the way he said it, I knew there were some. I was curious, and decided to piece together as much about Tripp as I could. As an acquaintance of his, I thought I could possibly detect something before the newspapers got hold of it and announced it to the world. Writing about one's friendship with a notable person is difficult: one wants to relate the story but remain in the background.

I spent several hours the next day in the local library researching the known life of Anthony Tripp. He was born in 1896, educated at Balliol, Oxford, and took his degree in 1925. He was invariably described as "a writer of popular fiction." His first novel was *The Lion's Roar*, published in 1947. He had been a lecturer and teacher. Since the appearance of *The Lion's Roar*, Tripp had written twenty-five novels, given speeches, received honorary doctorates and several book awards. Not a bad showing for someone who hadn't published a line until he was fifty-one years old.

There were enough gaps to create puzzles forever. Somehow, Tripp had managed to be a very private public man.

The attraction of other people's letters, whether for scholarly or self-seeking purposes, is one which is hard to resist. Perhaps it's the voyeur in each of us: we can peep through the key holes of time into the most interesting rooms in the world. Well-written, if not well-lived. Collected letters from time to time out-sell the actual literary works themselves. Perhaps there is more fact in fiction than fact in would-be fact.

I hadn't seen Tripp for several days when I visited him again. He was looking very ill. The sitting room was full of boxes, but everything was carefully arranged. I noticed that tags had been put on all the furniture.

"It's just like moving, only I won't have to unpack," he chuckled. He looked up from his chair. He had been reading a manuscript copy of what looked like a novel. "It won't be long now," he said. "I'm ready. All is in order."

I said nothing, but stood watching him.

He called me a lazy writer and he asked me to think about writing an article or two about him and his books. He said I would have access to all the notebooks, letters and journals in the college library.

He handed me the typescript he had been reading.

"This will explain a few things," he said. "Come back when you have finished reading it."

I took the typescript. The title page had three words on it: *Die Schöne Welt*. Another German story.

As soon as I got home, I read the manuscript. Then I re-read it the following day. His style had changed much in the years since he had penned *Die Schöne Welt*. The plot wasn't much, but its purpose was clear and it cast a new light on Anthony Tripp. One that would shock the world.

He met me two days later with an apologetic expression, such as one might have with a confessor. He was not immediately certain of my disposition.

I smiled.

"That's quite a bombshell," I said, handing him the manuscript.

"I expect you have much to ask," he said.

"I expect you have much to – "

"To answer for?"

"No, to tell."

"Sit down, and let us begin," he said.

"Is this to be a posthumous novel?" I asked.

"I haven't decided yet. It may be up to the college – or you," he said, before pausing. "You really don't know much about me, do you?"

"Less than I supposed. Though I have been doing some digging."

"Good. That is as it should be. But let me tell you, my friend, about myself and my *Schöne Welt*.

"As you can imagine, my name is not actually Anthony Tripp. What it is, or was, I don't think anyone will ever know for certain.

"I was born in Leipzig in 1896. I went to the local schools. I loved Goethe, Dante and Shakespeare. Shakespeare translates so well into German that it's difficult to believe it wasn't written that way.

"My greatest ambition was to become a poet. Heine and Hesse were just becoming known.

"My family was moderately wealthy. We had been unaffected by the Great War – well, nearly. We left everything and went to Russia, of all places. Father had a rich business associate who let us use his apartment in St. Petersburg. There was no language problem in Russia, we all spoke French. I actually saw the Tsar and Anastasia. Read the notebooks for more details.

"We stayed in Russia until the revolution was imminent. We left in time and began to search for a place to settle. Travel in Europe during the war was not difficult, as you would suppose, but we abandoned Europe and ended up in Bombay. We travelled as displaced White Russians.

"In India, we were no longer wealthy. Our Russian friends had left with only their lives and we carried our worn cases. I went to the English school in Bombay. Through friends and teachers there, I was accepted at Oxford. By the time I had been there a year, no one could tell I wasn't British. It was at Oxford I adopted the name of Tripp.

"At the end of *der erste Weltkrieg*, my father had gone back to Leipzig. Our Russian friends stayed in Bombay. Using our new contacts in India, father reorganized the business."

It was dark in Tripp's sitting room now. I felt I should leave, but wanted to hear the rest of his story. I told him that he shouldn't tire himself and that I would return the following day.

There was nothing in any of Tripp's books that suggested this experience. It was the sort of life that writers dream of; but to have it, and not be able to use it must have been enormously frustrating.

Still, there were things which he could not reveal. I dreamt of some forbidden love in the last days of the tsarist court.

I wrote down as much as I could remember and began to plan an article. Would it be possible to trace anything in Germany? India? Russia? It seemed rather improbable that any records would survive, especially if I didn't know his real name. And there was no indication that he planned to tell me that. Tripp was in a sea of paper when I saw him the next day.

"I found two stories this morning. I had forgotten about them. One in French from the time in Russia and the other in German. They're not very good, I'm afraid. Read them after I'm gone, then throw them away."

He resumed his story.

"I remember writing in Russia. I didn't take it very seriously. I expect we were living too comfortably. Critics still don't feel that I take writing seriously enough. But, remember Mr. Sleary in *Hard Times*? 'People mutht be amuthed'?"

"I always wanted to be a teacher at some great university. Heidelberg, Weimar, Oxford – nearly anywhere that I could lead a peaceful life and teach. By then, I had concluded that writing only interested me as a pastime.

"How far did we get yesterday?"

I told him.

"I had great fun at Oxford. I did feel that I had missed the great age and didn't think much of the post-war crowd. Still, I entertained well and fell in love several times. I wanted to continue with research, but things were happening in the Fatherland. My own father died in 1926 and I was called to run the business. Do I strike you as an indigo dealer? I did it rather well. Eventually, I sold the business to the government. This was 1935 – they were socialists, after all. It would only be a matter of time before they just took it."

He scanned my face for a reaction.

I gave none.

"My mind was not idle during the years I ran the business. I wrote articles on art and music and wrote a number of short stories – the short story is not so bad a form as I like to let on. They were published by odd, forgotten magazines, but they were not unnoticed.

"Not long after I sold the company, I received a letter from one Karl Hanke. He told me that he liked my work and would I come to Grunewald to discuss it. I went there and found a huge villa in the process of modernization, I discovered it was frequently used for party meetings in the district.

"Hanke and I sat in a large yellow office and he outlined an intriguing plan. He asked if I would be willing to help the government. How could I refuse? In those days, there was little reason – that we knew of – to refuse.

"He outlined a scheme to show Europe, in gentle ways, the benefits of the new Germany. Several weeks later, I sent Hanke a story. He accepted it and asked for more. The financial reward was good, and I had done well on the sale of the business. As time passed, things began to look more ominous.

I had been contemplating a trip abroad, to England, but Hanke was made State Secretary for the Ministry of Propaganda and he asked me to be one of his aides. The taste of honey – and power – was stronger than the urge to travel.

"I was given a great suite in Berlin and there was plenty of art, music and entertainment. I edited a magazine which eventually was to have worldwide distribution. It was a vehicle to spread the word of the cause and to win support for our philosophy. The magazine ran until 1944 with a monthly circulation of five million.

"When the war began, Hitler's plan for the new Berlin and other model cities took shape. Karl had the idea for a series of futuristic novels to bolster the people's morale and strengthen their faith in the war effort. By the direct request of Dr. Goebbels, I met with Albert Speer to discuss the physical aspects of the new Berlin. I was to write a novel about life in the near utopian city."

"*Die Schöne Welt*?"

"*Die Schöne Welt.*

I looked at the typescript on the table.

"It's the first novel I ever wrote. Its German version is around somewhere. It was to be printed, shipped to Britain, America and distributed all over Europe to encourage sympathizers there.

"By the time the book was finished, printing novels – even for propaganda purposes – wasn't a priority. To anyone who knew what was going on, it was clear that the war was lost. The problem became one of how to get off the ship before it sank without being shot for mutiny. I requested travel permits from the Ministry. They were denied.

"I was scared. I packed a suitcase once again. I had mailed much to England in the early thirties when I had expected to do research after selling the business.

"I had to get to Switzerland. I wrote travel letters on Ministry stationery and bullied officials into letting me out. I told them I was distributing propaganda. I was, too: to them.

"Switzerland had a clever network for refugees. It was difficult at first because no one wanted to trust me. I was immediately missed in Berlin. I was nearly arrested in Africa. Eventually, I made my way to England, the day of the Battle of the Bulge. I lived with Oxford friends, who thought I was just back from Bombay. Gradually, I merged back into British society. It wasn't difficult with the friends I had there. I undertook work first with the Civil Defence Service. No one knew who was dead or alive and records were lost daily. Claim that your home was bombed and who would know that you had just arrived?

"My German colleagues were either executed or jailed; some committed suicide, others moved to South America. None of those who survived ever suspected that their old friend from the Ministry of Propaganda was living openly as the English novelist, Anthony Tripp.

"I was afraid that Speer might remember me and say something when he published his memoirs a few years back. I had been safe for so long but never without fear. Would Borman come out of the jungle and say, 'Anthony Tripp is an ex-Nazi propagandist'?

"Somehow, I feel I have paid for it all. In two ways: first, as a writer who couldn't write his greatest book; and secondly, as a man who has never been free from fear.

"Once, you asked what my favorite novel was. Can you guess now? There is always something special about your first."

Cߦ

It was the last time I saw Tripp alive. When I called

round the next day, he was dead. A neighbor who helped him up in the morning had found him. He'd been taken away, and the house sealed by the police.

I began my work immediately. I searched the libraries for information on the Nazi Propaganda Ministry. I wrote Oxford and Bombay. I wrote historians to see if any of them knew of Hanke's plan for novels. None of them even knew of the mass-circulation magazines.

As soon as Tripp's will had been probated and his papers transferred to the college, I went to the library to begin work. The boxes were in the process of being cataloged and in exchange for previews of the contents, I helped with the process.

Rosie Graves was the assistant librarian that I worked with. She had met Tripp on several occasions when he'd visited the college to speak to a senior seminar or use the library.

"One of my good friends, Janet Montgomery, is married to Anthony Tripp's doctor," she prattled as we worked. "She says that Tripp was drugged to the eyeballs for the pain. It was a wonder he was able to function at all at home."

"He needed help with many things, but was pretty good. Sharp, too."

"Was he?" she stopped sorting a stack of letters. "Janet said he barely knew if it was day or night towards the end. She said that her husband had told her all sorts of things he'd made up."

I told her that had not been my experience. I was glad that I had my hands on the papers and would soon be able to prove it, too.

We went through box after box containing proof copies, scrapbooks of reviews and notices, copies of lectures and talks, diplomas for honorary degrees, letters from his publishers and agents, cancelled checks, and utility bills. The journals he had spoken about were there too, but they began in 1948, and there was no copy, nor mention of *Die Schöne Welt*.

"Gossip"

Thoughts and Whispers

"Gossip"

I t couldn't have happened at a worse time. I was in a hurry; I needed to concentrate, and I needed the meeting I was headed to to go well.

I'd come up on the train to Charing Cross and due to disruptions on the Underground, decided to walk from there to my meeting near Grosvenor Square. Over Pall Mall; up St James'; across Piccadilly, and up Bond Street would do it.

It was nearly a year since I set up on my own after decades of working for other people. It was going well, but today's meeting was going to make a big difference. An international customer I'd been in touch with for a long time was now ready to act, and my fledgling business was ready to take on work of the scale I hoped would be offered.

As I walked up the streets, my head was going through all the things we needed to talk about, and I was running through the check-list of files on my tablet. They were all on the drive as well as in the Cloud; I wasn't taking any chances.

I was just about confident that all was in order as I exited Burlington Arcade and moved into Bond Street. I relaxed, slowed my pace, took some deep breaths and took more notice of my surroundings.

Bond Street is an extraordinary place with extravagant rents and goods of all description commanding prices that matched. These shops and galleries needed to achieve their rent figures in the first week of each month, otherwise, unless they had serious backing, they'd be in trouble. Few people appreciate that many of these top names are on as much of a shoe-string as a small family business. Only the numbers are bigger.

It was probably only the third window I looked in, towards the northern end of Old Bond Street, that a painting in a gallery caught my eye.

It was a small, domestic-scale oil painting measuring about 30 x 50cm with a plain gilt frame. It dated from the second half of the 19th century and showed two fashionably dressed women, with furs and feathered hats, sitting at a café table, engrossed in friendly discussion. The background was dark, but there was the suggestion of bottles, crockery and glass, and the ghost of an aproned waiter loomed in the shadows. The women's faces were brightly lit and animated in a conversation you could almost hear. One of them was leaning forward, eager to hear what the other said, while the second woman had the attitude of one enjoying being the centre of attention and the source of information. One elbow rested on the table, and the hand that was near her face held a coffee spoon almost vertically, with the tip of the bowl pointing downwards.

I came to such an abrupt stop that two women behind me, who themselves had been engaged in conversation, walked into me at full speed. We apologised with the perfunctory gabble, and they moved on while I remained, my eyes fixed on the picture.

The sight of a man moving towards the picture within the gallery brought me back to reality. He, no doubt, had come to mentally record a full description of me should the painting prove not to be there one morning.

I gathered my thoughts and continued to the meeting, which I now had less interest in, because the sight of the painting had unleashed a flood of memories from thirty years before.

You see, I once lived in the house where that painting had hung.

ભ

My meeting, while not perfect, went well enough. At one point, my potential client asked if everything was all right. I managed to say that I'd just learned my non-existent brother was very ill on travels in the Far East. Even though it was a lie, acknowledging the distraction served to bring things back into focus. The meeting went well after that, and the prospect suggested we go for lunch.

Even in my eagerness to get back to the gallery, I could see this was too good an opportunity to miss. It was a good thing, too, as we both relaxed, and when we parted two hours later, the deal was pretty much agreed; he even wished my brother a speedy recovery.

I made my way back to Bond Street and Galèries Concorde and after assuring myself that this was, indeed, the picture I knew, I went in.

Well, I tried to.

Why it is that galleries think they have to be intimidating has always mystified me. After all, they are selling things that are quite useless and of little intrinsic value. Sought after and expensive, but useless. The London branch of Galèries Concorde had taken customer intimidation to a new level, as when I pushed on the gold and glass door, it was locked. Presumably the Paris, New York, Los Angeles and Buenos Aires branches were busy enough to subsidise this rude and empty shop.

A skeletal girl with long straight hair and wearing a suit and scarf that probably cost a month's rent for the premises tottered up to the door.

"Do you want to see something?" she asked through the glass.

"No, I just like walking into locked doors," I said, loudly enough that a few people near me could hear.

I stepped back from the door and waited. The spectre turned and went to a glass-topped trestle table to the rear of the gallery and took a key on a long red ribbon from a silver box and returned to the door.

She unlocked it with a bit of trouble that damaged her pretence of cool efficiency. Eventually, she succeeded, and restored the *status frigidum* by returning to the desk to put the key back in the box, leaving me to open the door myself.

"How can I help you?" she asked the back wall.

I didn't reply and waited until she was facing me and I had moved to within six feet.

"When will the manager be in?" I asked politely.

Her eyes immediately dilated, and nostrils that were probably no stranger to cocaine (and now incapable of flaring) twitched.

"What makes you think I'm not the manager?" she asked pointedly, but not too aggressively.

"You don't act like one."

"Monsieur Brogan will be back by four," she replied.

She was about to continue but I spoke first.

"You may tell him that I'm interested in the painting in the window."

"The 19th century French piece? It's attributed to Jean Bérnaud," she said, implying I could never afford it.

"1880s," I said.

I handed her a business card.

"I'll be back at four," I said.

She looked at the card and decided it was worth

walking to the front door with me.

When I set up my business, I decided that for the purposes of the website, letterhead and business cards that a good name, a distinguished font and outstanding paper was worth the investment. "Stirling-Brooke, London, Paris & New York" looked and felt good on a thick ivory card, and belied the fact that I was, in reality, a sole trader, but with a worldwide network of people I could call who worked on a project basis.

Two can play this game, Galèries Concorde.

CR

I spent the next hour browsing in Burlington Arcade. Like Bond Street, it wasn't a place where many mere mortals spent their money, but I had bought my wife's engagement ring there many years ago, and, when I'd received a bonus, a pair of antique gold cufflinks for myself (which mysteriously show up on my son's cuffs from time to time).

I walked down Piccadilly to Hatchard's, reviewing what I remembered about the painting, which wasn't much. I also needed to clarify what I wanted from the discussion with Monsieur Brogan at the gallery. I couldn't afford to buy it, but I would like to re-connect with the owner – or at least the owners I remembered.

It had been a very happy time, until it wasn't.

The door was unlocked when I returned to Galèries Concorde. The creature was cataloguing something at the glass desk and gave Monsieur Brogan a slight nod when I entered.

"Mr Brooke, I'm sorry I wasn't here when you came by," he said.

He was pleasant, but formal. He wore an expensive well-cut suit with a blue and white striped shirt and lions head cufflinks made of what looked like marble. A perfect gallery confection, not too formal, not too trendy; not too familiar and struggling not to be too judgemental.

"I understand you want to talk about the Bérnaud," he said.

I looked him squarely in the eye for just long enough to make him blink.

"No, I want to talk about the painting in the window."

He glanced back at the creature who was keeping her head down.

"Let's go into my office; it will be more comfortable there," he said. "Thank you, Francesca."

The office was behind a wall of plate glass that had frosted effects that suggested a Rousseau jungle. A large oriental rug covered most of the floor. At one end, there was another glass trestle table with two Wassily chairs before it, and a round table with four less distinguished, and less comfortable chairs. Clusters of LED spotlights were casting cones of light randomly.

I moved around the table to sit facing the front of the shop, at ninety degrees to where he was going to sit. I could see his hesitation before he reluctantly moved to sit with his back to the show room, across from me. I'd made the move with a calculated bit of bumbling, taking the seat as if by awkward accident, but I wasn't sure he bought it.

When we were both seated, he returned to the painting.

"Are you a collector, Mr Brooke?" he asked with casual calculation.

"Not usually," I admitted. "I've picked up a few things over the years, but I look a lot."

"Were you questioning the authenticity of the Bérnaud?" he asked as politely as he could.

I decided to change tack.

"I came in to find out how you happened to be selling the picture," I said. "I once lived in the house where it used to hang."

Monsieur Brogan, who was not French, but came from the north side of Limerick (wonderful thing, the internet) was clearly considering what to say next.

He stood and went to one of the file cabinets and unlocked it. He drew out a file that contained an A4 manila envelope.

"You're a business man," he began, sitting down again. "You will appreciate that I can't tell you where I got the picture from. Galleries depend on trust, expertise and documentation."

"Yes, and we all know that about fifty per cent of everything sold at auction is fake," I said.

He said nothing, and was working harder to hide his discomfort.

"You asked my interest in the piece. Well, I'll tell you," I said. "The lady who owned it was my landlady nearly thirty years ago. It was on the wall in her hallway when I rented upstairs rooms from her.

"All I will tell you at this stage," I continued, "that might help you validate your paperwork is that the owner lived in the Home Counties, and her surname was a well-known household brand name, though there was no connection."

Brogan put the envelope back in the folder and closed it.

"What I have been told, and the documents I have state, is that the picture came from a house sale outside Paris last year," he said. "It came to us having first been shown in our Paris gallery. If it doesn't sell here within three months, it will go to New York."

"Thirty years is a long time. It wasn't inconceivable that it went to France with a member of her family; or it could have been sold with her effects," I said. "There's no doubt that my old landlady is dead by now. Had it been placed with you by one of her heirs, I would have asked that you give them my details as I would like to re-establish contact. That's my total interest – though I do like the painting but I should tell you that the painting wasn't attributed to Bérnaud then."

I stood up.

"You have given me a bit of a problem," Brogan said. "I will look into this. Most of the records are at our head office in Paris."

"You have my card. I could give you more details of the owner and her family, which might help."

"I understand," he said.

I had my hand on the office door, but before I opened it, Brogan asked:

"Why do you doubt it's a Bérnaud?"

"He did do a few things of that intimacy, but he generally painted grander scenes and used more colour," I said, my time in Hatchard's having been well spent. "That picture was smuggled out of Europe in the 1920s, and the painter was Polish. It's called 'Gossip'."

ଓଃ

On the train home, I reflected that Brogan hadn't reacted quite the way I thought he would. He was clearly rattled. Had he suspected other works?

I had what I wanted, or not, as it turned out. I wanted to re-establish contact with the Liptons, and that didn't look like happening via Galèries Concorde. Besides, I had my new project to think about, and what I did was a long way from the art world.

By the time I reached home, I had decided there was nothing to be done about the painting; I wasn't going to buy it, so how it was attributed was nothing to do with me, besides, my knowledge of art was superficial. As for the Liptons, I had no real reason, apart from general curiosity, to get back in touch with them. That and the question about 'Gossip.'

My first job had taken me from the rural comforts of Hereford to dull, but promising work in the even more dull, and less promising, Crawley. One of the managers at the company told me that the chap I was replacing – who had left to do something more exciting and lucrative in the City – had digs in a large house belonging to a widow, in a nicer part of Sussex, that I might take over.

I arranged to visit Mrs Trevelyan at her home on a mature, wooded plot. It was a large Victorian house on a street of similar properties, some of which had been converted into flats.

When we met, we hit it off as well as my predecessor had done and I took up occupancy. Mrs Trevelyan lived on the ground floor, and I had two rooms and a private bath on the first floor. She had a study/workroom up there, too, but tended to use it in the daytime, so I had satisfactory privacy.

We shared the kitchen and occasional meals. She

was a fit and active seventy-three and was seldom in. She was active in her church, the WI, the local Tory party, a bridge club, and a garden club. Those, along with a variety of charitable organisations, and the widower next door and his family, occupied most of her time.

She was well-read and well-travelled and could talk intelligently on a wide range of subjects.

Over the five years I lived there, I came to know her life story and met most of her family.

Mrs Trevelyan was British, having been born of English parents in Poland, while her father was developing oil wells in the Carpathian Mountains. The market collapsed and they returned to England bringing with them a fair amount of silver, some china, a pile of Russian sables and half a dozen paintings.

Mrs Trevelyan had been the wife of a Royal Navy officer who had been a young lieutenant during the war but retired as an admiral. He held several corporate directorships and advised the Admiralty and the Department of Defence until his early death, aged 69.

I didn't remember Mrs Trevelyan's maiden name, but her sister, Monica, had married Jerzy Liptowsky, a refugee who had worked with their father in Poland. On arrival in the UK, he became George Lipton, and later Sir George. Lady Monica had the same sense of mischievous fun as her sister, and I had met them in

London once by accident and, after having tea at Fortnum & Mason, Lady Monica stepped to the kerb on Piccadilly, put two fingers in her mouth and gave an ear-splitting whistle that immediately summoned a taxi.

Sir George had fallen off the twig a decade before I met Lady Monica, but I did meet their grown children, and grandchildren who were around my age. It would be one of them that I would attempt to find.

ဆ

I should explain my domestic arrangements. I am a widower. My son is grown and working in London. I am living in the house my wife and I shared, but now share it with my sister who moved in after her divorce. She is very practical and between her own work – which she does at home – she keeps the garden tamed and the house in order, though I do my share. My sister had no interest in art and thought I was wasting my time pretending to. She wasn't at all interested that I'd identified a misattributed painting in Bond Street, but wanted to know every detail of my meeting and what needed to be done to secure the hoped for business.

I got the message, and didn't bother her with talk of Brogan, Francesca, Bérnaud, or Mrs Trevelyan. She was only interested in any renewed contact with the Liptons if they presented possibilities for new romantic interests for either of us.

The Liptons had been an attractive family, and there

was almost some history there, which made me both wary and intrigued by the possibility of renewed contact. Inevitably, I Googled them and checked LinkedIn for the members of my generation (Sir George's and Lady Monica's grandchildren). Remembering their names was the biggest challenge. I eventually got them: Henry (who was married to Petra), Peter, Arabella, and Sally. I remembered very little about some of them, or which of Lady Monica's sons were their fathers. Lady Monica also had an unmarried daughter, Caroline, I think. She was a favourite of the grandchildren because of her directness and brutal irony. I was fond of her, too, though I only met her two or three times. Of the ones of my generation, I remember liking Peter; wanting to be liked by Henry, who regarded me as a hanger-on; and Arabella, whom I liked very much, but hardly dared to speak to as she was only in her first year of university when I met her. Her older sister, Sally, was another story. Suffice to say that she was one of those rare women who make a room fall silent when they walk in.

Sir George had been successful in manufacturing electronic components. One or more of his sons had helped moved the business into computer hardware and software in the 1960s. From what I learned on the web, the company continued, still in family ownership, and manufacturing components for the major computer suppliers.

I found Peter's name as CFO on one of the group's companies, still based in Sussex, and noted the telephone number. Others I couldn't find, and others were based abroad.

I had no reason to contact any of them, but felt at least I would be able to.

Shortly after supper Sunday night, I closed my laptop and settled back to finish the bottle of wine and watch television.

I missed the end of the film because my business mobile rang a few minutes after nine.

"Mr Brooke, this is Dermot Brogan from Galèries Concorde. I am sorry to bother you at home on Sunday night, but is there any chance you could meet me tomorrow afternoon, around two o'clock at the bar on the upper level of Waterloo station?"

There was no point asking if it were important as his voice said it all.

"I can do that," I said.

"Good. Thank you," he said and rang off.

At my age, what chance does one get for a bit of adventure?

శం

I was able to get some work done on the train from Lewes and the change to Waterloo was easy. The morning had been busy so I barely had time for "Gossip," as it were. There was no reason to tell my sister that my trip to London was for anything but business.

As expected, the bar was heaving with office workers and travellers. If Brogan were already there, I expected he'd be watching the bar and not the perimeter of the crowd, so I made my way to the bar and picked up a plastic cup of red wine. When I had it and stepped back, I saw Brogan.

"Thank you for coming," he said, his Irish accent showing through more today.

He was similarly dressed to Friday, but his manner wasn't as assured.

We moved away from the bar to a quieter area between two shops. After two sips, I dumped the drink.

"After you left on Friday, I called Paris and simply reported that we'd had a question about the provenance of the picture," he said. "I gave no names; no details, but merely asked for verification and a copy of any evidence they had. It was a routine request, and a cordial conversation."

He paused.

"Last night, about ten minutes before I called you, I had a call from one of the directors in Paris saying that the gallery was undergoing a reorganisation and that I'd get details this morning," he said. "It was a lot to ask you to meet me, but I got the feeling that things would be happening fast. And they did."

Brogan was nervously scanning the crowd, and we

began to walk down the concourse, pausing in quiet spots for a few moments before moving on.

"When I got to the gallery this morning, the painting, 'Gossip', wasn't in the window. In fact, it was no longer in the gallery," he said.

"Was it stolen?" I asked, surprised by this revelation.

"No," he said. "Francesca must have made a quick trip to Paris on Saturday. I think she took it back to the main gallery, but that's just a guess. I suspect it's on its way to New York or Los Angeles now."

"Not Buenos Aires?" I asked, remembering the list of cities on the window.

"No, that's where I'm going," Brogan said. "That is, if I decide to remain with the organisation."

"They're transferring you?" I asked, surprised, suddenly very worried about what I had started. "I'm sorry," I stammered.

Brogan gave an easy grin.

"Not your fault. You asked a perfectly legitimate question," he said. "You are not the first to have done so in my time at the gallery. I have seen some suspect things come in, but they were moved on without causing problems."

We'd reached the end of the concourse and turned to walk back.

"And does Francesca have the authority to remove pictures from the gallery – and the country? I thought you were the manager."

"And so did I," Brogan said. "But that's not the way things work at Galèries Concorde. Francesca has a special connection with the directors. You probably noticed that she's not the most amiable of colleagues."

I returned his hint of a smile.

"That sort of attitude is not unusual when one first walks into a gallery," he said. "They like to intimidate, especially in London where they like keeping the out-crowd out. They tend to know more about art and ask too many questions. Hardly egalitarian."

"You've worked in galleries for a while," I said.

"For about fifteen years. In Dublin mostly, then a few years in Paris. That was where I was approached by Galèries Concorde," he said, smiling. "So, yes; I know how things should be done."

"So where do you go from here? How's your Spanish?"

His smile was now gone.

"It's probably best that I don't tell you yet," he said. "To be honest, I'm not altogether sure. I know you said your connections with the picture were old, but if you could find out what happened to it when it left your landlady's, it could give a starting point – an auction, or something. If you can't, well, you can't."

"I'll see what I can do."

He nodded.

"Most likely, this is a one-off cock-up of some sort, but I don't think that would result in sending me to Argentina," he said. "As you said, fifty per cent of all art sold is fake."

He gave me a private email address and shook my hand.

"Good luck."

"You, too."

&

Work had to come first and there was a lot of it, but on Thursday afternoon, I called LPT Systems and asked to speak to Peter Lipton. The receptionist had sounded efficient, but friendly and I had a similar impression when put through to his PA.

"I'm sorry Mr Brooke, but Peter's out today. May I help with something, or leave him a message?"

"It's a personal matter; I'm an old family friend," I said. "I've been out of touch for a long time."

"Sophie – Mrs Lipton – is here; I can put you through to her."

I was transferred before I could protest.

I explained my connection and named a few people in the family. Peter had married after I'd moved away.

"I'm afraid I never met Mrs Trevelyan, or Lady Monica," Sophie said easily. "I have heard lots of stories, and gather that they were both unconventional even when in their eighties."

I told her that I'd seen one of Mrs Trevelyan's paintings, mis-identified, in a gallery and would Peter know anything about where it went after her death?

"Peter was in Dubai at the time," Sophie said. "He came back for the funeral, but then went straight out again."

I paused wondering what to ask next. I didn't want to give the impression I wanted anything except my curiosity satisfied.

"When it comes to the antiques and pictures, you should talk to Arabella," Sophie volunteered. "She handled all of that for Mrs Trevelyan, Lady Monica and Peter's father. None of us was around, or had any interest. Did you know Arabella?"

I explained she was a teenager when I'd last seen her.

"She's very grown up now – well, most of the time," Sophie laughed.

She gave me her email address and a telephone number.

Sophie's open, trusting manner reflected how I remembered the Liptons. Even though she had married into the family, it was obvious even from that short conversation that she shared their characteristics. As for telephoning Arabella – I'd have to think about that for a while.

She hadn't married, which given her looks and

personality during her time at Oxford, was something of a mystery.

ᔥ

I hadn't asked Sophie for any family details, but I did wonder about Arabella's older sister, Sally. Sally was close to my age, and she had invited me on a few precarious dates. I was just her great-aunt's lodger and not about to risk being evicted.

The first was a simple Saturday lunch at a country pub which extended until early evening when we both had other engagements. The second time was a casual dinner, again at a pub. We sat outside until we were getting not too subtle hints about leaving.

We telephoned nearly every day until the following weekend when Sally was having a dinner party and invited me. It was the normal progression of decades ago when two people didn't live close and were busy establishing careers. A dinner party was a little more serious, and I feared her friends would clearly be of a wholly different type to me: bankers, lawyers, or art dealers, like Sally.

I put on a tie, bought a decent bottle and headed off.

While there were lights on at Sally's ground floor apartment, it was clear that I was the first to arrive, even though it was fifteen minutes after the stated time.

She welcomed me. The presence of good furniture and pictures was immediately evident. The sitting room had a warm, welcoming glow. Music played at just the right volume in the background. While a comfortable room, I sensed that all had been carefully calculated. She chatted easily, took the bottle to the kitchen and shortly returned with an opened bottle, two glasses and a bowl of nuts and one of olives.

She sat in the opposite corner of the sofa to me, but had her back against the arm, so she faced me squarely.

"Dinner party?" I asked tentatively.

"Did I say party?" she said with affected vagueness. "I meant dinner."

She had cooked an excellent, sophisticated meal after which we retired to the sitting room, and she curled up with me and a brandy. It was then she told me her fiancé was returning late the next afternoon.

I haven't seen her since.

It was one of the reasons I hesitated to call either of the girls.

There was no word from Brogan by close of business Wednesday afternoon. I didn't know what that meant, but thought that if he did get in touch, I ought to have something to tell him, so I called Arabella in the early evening.

"I was wondering when I was going to hear from you," Arabella said when I told her who I was. "Sophie said she'd given you my number."

"And had second thoughts about doing so?" I said.

"Yes, but I told her it was all right," she said with a laugh. "Look. I'm just on my way out. Do you still stay up late? Like eleven?"

"I'm not all that much older than you," I said.

"You used to think so," she retorted. "I'll call as near to eleven as possible."

I had always thought there was a "Lipton manner." Not all of them had it, but there was that certain something, and it immediately revealed itself in Arabella. Part of it was the ability to pick up with someone one hadn't spoken to in twenty-five years. It was something I knew I could do, and was pleased to do so, but I am always surprised when others can do it, too.

Very shortly after eleven, Arabella called.

"A friend of mine was in a play in Brighton," she said. "Am-dram of the worst sort, I'm afraid, but my friend was very good. I'd love to see her in something decent, but as a housewife and mother what chance has she got?

"You didn't call me after all this time to hear about Brenda," she said. "What have I done now?"

I laughed.

"I saw one of your Aunt Sibyl's pictures in a Bond Street Gallery last week. It was mis-identified as French."

"Which one?" she asked.

"'Gossip.'"

The line was very quiet.

"Arabella?"

"I think we'd better meet," she said, her voice almost a whisper. "Can you do the Norfolk Arms tomorrow night at seven? It's a mutually inconvenient location."

ℭℛ

It was not only an inconvenient location, but an inconvenient day. After daydreaming about the Liptons, "Gossip" and my time at Mrs Trevelyan's, on the way to work, the day was full-on with strategy planning, conference calls, budgeting and the usual daily brushfires that all businesses face. By the time I lifted my eyes out of the ledger, it was past the time I had intended to head to Arundel. The A27 would be a nightmare; overtaking was impossible for long stretches. I didn't have a mobile number for Arabella, so all I could do is set off and hope for the best.

I was twenty minutes late by the time I walked into the bar of the Norfolk Arms. Though the hotel looked familiar, the bar had been given an upgrade which I only disliked because it wasn't the same as I remembered.

I ordered a large glass of red and found a seat in what I hoped would remain a quiet corner. Several locals were at the bar finishing their pints, and a few couples were having a drink while reading large menus, presumably for the dining room.

I was reading a business magazine, something I usually didn't have time for. I was engrossed in a story of a company that developed a new fuel made from cocoa bean husks when Arabella strode up to the table.

"I'm sorry I'm so late," she said as I stood up. "I've come from Salisbury and the traffic – "

"That's even more inconvenient than Lewes," I said.

She gave me a big hug, then kissed my cheeks.

"It's so good to see old friends."

Is that what we were?

She sat down and divested herself of a smart shabby chic denim jacket and a large leather handbag that hung by a thick strap.

"I'd forgotten I was going there," she continued. "The run from Godalming wouldn't have been too bad."

I brought her a glass of the same red I was drinking. She took a modest mouthful.

"That's actually not bad," she said.

"I expect anything would taste good just now."

Now in her mid-forties, Arabella still had the mannerisms and bearing that I remembered from when I'd met her.

"Golly! You're thinking just how much I've gone off since we first met," she said, with an unmistakable Katherine Hepburn voice.

"I was thinking you looked fantastic."

"Well preserved, you mean?" she retorted.

"Don't be difficult," I said. "Do you want something to eat?"

"Yes, but let me catch my breath, and let's start to catch up," she said.

"What are you doing now?" we asked simultaneously, then laughed.

"Oh, dear," she said. "This is rather like a computer date."

"Is it?" I asked with a straight face.

She laughed.

"I wouldn't know, either," she said.

I glanced at her left hand; she saw me.

"No, no luck there."

She didn't look particularly unhappy.

"I'm still in the antiques business," she said. "I was looking at a few pieces today that the owners thought were original Chippendale. So I drove all the way out to find 'Gillow' punched on the underside of a drawer.

"That's pretty typical of the way I spend my life," she sighed.

I told her what I did, and repeated what I had told her on the telephone about the painting.

"How amazing to come across it after all these years. Well done for recognising it," she said.

"So do you know more about it, and how it came to be in Bond Street?" I asked.

"May I have another glass of this, please?" she said. "And can you ask for menus. Just the bar menu."

We looked at the menu as she worked her way

through her second glass. We both opted for the Sri Lankan goat curry, which I ordered at the bar.

"Sally is looking forward to seeing you," she said, when I sat back down.

"And when is she going to see me?"

"When she comes over from Paris to talk to you – unless you'd like to go there. She said that would be all right, too," Arabella said.

I considered this.

"Did Sally – "

"She's Priscilla now; she's grown up," Arabella said ironically. "That's what she likes to be called."

"Well, that's not going to happen," I said.

Arabella laughed.

"I still call her Sally, too," she said.

"Did she tell you what happened the last time I saw her?" I asked.

"Oh, yes. I think she told everyone," Arabella said. "She cooked you a gourmet meal, and everything was going well, and then you suddenly ran away."

Arabella's tone wasn't judgemental; she was just relating a family story.

"Did she mention the part when she told me her fiancé was arriving the next day?"

"What fiancé? She wasn't engaged to anyone then," Arabella said, with a big grin.

"I guess she was trying to get rid of me," I said,

miffed at how I'd been portrayed in the Lipton family for a generation.

Arabella giggled.

"Poor Gregory," she said. "You didn't deserve that. We all rather liked you."

"She didn't have to do it that way," I said.

"Oh, you fool. She was trying to get you to say there was no one for her but you."

I shrugged.

"I'm sorry; I didn't think that then, and I don't think that now," I said.

"I know," Arabella said in a low, dark voice. "*Are* you married?"

"If I said yes, would you believe me?"

She burst out laughing.

Our meal came. After eating and talking about the food, the hotel and general things, I returned to "Gossip."

"Sally handled Aunt Sibyl's pictures," she said. "She left everything to be split between her nephews and niece. It was all very simple and clear. The cash and securities after the sale of the house were divided evenly. They had first pick of everything, one choice at a time by age, and anything left was to be sold or given away – their choice – and any money divided equally.

"Well, most of them had a houseful of furniture already," she said. "They chose things for my generation, but there was quite a lot that no one had room for or wanted. I have to say that there were things I wish I had now."

"And no one wanted 'Gossip'?"

"You'd think someone would," Arabella said. "One of us would have loved it, but our fathers didn't and that's what decided it. I was given the furniture to sell, and Sally the paintings.

"There were a few tables and chairs I wanted, and I asked my father and uncles to set a price, and bought them. One or two of the others did the same, but most weren't interested in buying things."

She ate some more goat.

"So Sally got 'Gossip' to sell?"

Arabella nodded.

"I'm sorry we lost touch with you," she said *á propos* of nothing. "Aunt Sibyl was very fond of you – and so was I."

"I must have been insufferable," she said, after a moment's reflection.

"But very pretty."

She looked disappointed that I hadn't contradicted her, but accepted the complimentary part.

"So, when did Sally sell 'Gossip'?" I asked, returning to safer ground.

Arabella shook her head.

"I have no idea," she said. "She took possession of it about a year after Aunt Sibyl died; that was eighteen years ago. She could have held it for market reasons, or she could have sold it right away. That's why you need to talk to her."

I nodded.

"I haven't told you the next part of my story," I said. "I wanted to talk to you before telling you, but Brogan, the manager at Bond Street, was transferred to South America."

"When?" Arabella asked, surprised.

"Over the weekend," I said. "And the painting is no longer in the gallery."

"But why?"

"I was hoping you or your sister could tell me," I said. "Brogan indicated that this was not the first time he'd questioned a picture."

Arabella put her knife and fork down. She looked worried for the first time.

"Sally is involved with Galèries Concorde," she said softly. "Her ex-husband is the managing director."

I waited for a moment in case she was going to say anything more.

"She might still do some work with them."

I stopped eating.

"Arabella, I don't have to go any further with this," I said. "I stumbled into it and was curious. That's all. It's nothing to do with my work; I have no intention of buying it. Whatever anyone wants to do is fine with me.

Though Brogan struck me as a decent guy in the end."

"Did you see anyone else at the gallery?" Arabella asked. I sensed she wanted me to say, "No."

"Only a pretentious assistant called Francesca, who I think was really more than just someone's assistant," I said.

Arabella laughed.

"Ha! The stick-insect. Sally's ex-sister-in-law."

I wiped my lips and threw my napkin on the table.

"That's it; I'm done. I'm not getting involved in this any further."

We had coffee and spoke of other things. I told her about living with my sister and my new venture. Arabella was curious about my business and I asked her about antique shows, auctions and a few of her other relatives.

When we'd finished and I walked with her to her car, she took my arm.

"Don't give up on this. Talk to Sally when she gets here. She's not had an easy time of it; she'll be able to answer your questions."

I was quiet for a minute, and she squeezed my arm.

"Please."

"I'll think about it," I said eventually.

I wasn't happy about any of this.

She got in the car and rolled the window down when I'd shut the door.

"Can I see you again?"

"I'll think about that too," I said and went to my car.

It was the sense of being played that put me off. Arabella and Sally knew something, and while I didn't think Arabella knew the whole story, she knew more than she told me. If I was ever going to know the truth I would have to find it somewhere else, but just then, I no longer cared.

℘

Two weeks passed. Work was going well. New projects were underway for our new client. "Gossip" and the Liptons had receded to the back of my mind and with the distance, I was starting to regret treating Arabella as I had. It had been good to see her. It had resolved things, after a fashion, and while I could see much of the young girl I knew, I didn't want to be drawn in.

That was my position when Arabella telephoned one evening. Her voice was friendly, and she didn't mention the chilly way I'd left her in Arundel.

"Sally arrives tomorrow," she said. "When she calls you, please talk to her. See her. It will be best."

I said nothing.

"I do care," Arabella whispered before hanging up.

I was in a meeting when Sally telephoned. Really. Apparently, she didn't query it and left a message for me to meet her the next day at two o'clock in the foyer of the Royal Academy of Arts. She declined to leave a number, email or address.

I went, and was sitting on one of the benches in the window when she swept in, elegant long coat flapping and a colourful scarf tied loosely around her neck.

"Gregory!" she hove up, embraced me, and gave me a too-sustained kiss.

"You look wonderful," she gushed.

I didn't. She did.

"Come, let's get a drink."

We moved into the Friends' area, through the café and down the stairs to the bar. At this hour, it was relatively empty. She pointed to a corner of the banquette.

"Sit there."

She went to the bar and ordered some drinks in about five seconds, then came and sat at ninety degrees to me.

"I'm so excited to see you! Arabella said you'd had dinner together. I'll have to scratch her eyes out later," she said without pausing for breath.

"So, you've been making trouble for Galèries Concorde," she continued.

It wasn't a question.

"Not at all, it seems to have made trouble for itself," I said.

She still had the looks that could get her anything

she wanted.

Our drinks came along with a bowl of olives and some mixed nuts. Over the next few minutes, Sally picked out all the cashews and ate them.

"Business first," she said. "Then we can relax and catch up, and go for drinks and dinner."

"'Gossip'," I said.

"There was never any evidence of what the painting was called," Sally said.

"It was called *Gossip* when Mrs Trevelyan's father bought it."

"Family stories are wonderful, aren't they," she said. Then, held up her glass, "*Santé.*"

"*Twoje zdrowie.*"

"Very droll," she said before drinking.

She took a second drink, leaving her large glass half full. She leaned back against the banquette and sighed. She wasn't angry, unhappy, or even moderately displeased. She just looked weary.

"Darling, I know you knew us pretty well at one time, especially Aunt Sibyl; but families are complicated organisms, and sometimes in order to ensure their own survival, certain – *accommodations* – are made," she said.

I remembered how much I loved her voice. Round, rich, perfectly modulated and enunciated. She could lower the pitch and turn on the subtlest huskiness so easily.

"Sibyl's father, my great-grandfather, Marcus Michelsson, was, shall we say, an adventurer," she began. "You will know of their Middle European travels and the stories of oil wells, sables and escaping on sleighs. It's all true. By all accounts, he was an extraordinary man and had an army of friends.

"He wasn't a thief; he wasn't involved with Mafia-like organisations – apart from the British Secret Service, and that only occasionally. I don't think he ever did anyone real harm, and if the stories are true, he did a lot of good – if unconventionally."

She paused to take another drink, then waved to the bartender for two more glasses.

None of this about Mrs Trevelyan's father was unknown to me. No doubt he was a colourful character who sometimes took advantage of a situation; no more than other entrepreneurial adventurers of the day.

"All of this is at least third-hand, but it came from the Lipton side of the family (who, believe me, was less scrupulous), whereas, what you know is from Aunt Sibyl," Sally continued.

"There was always a risk that someone would recognise 'Gossip' if we tried to sell it in London," she resumed. "That was one of the reasons I waited so long before putting it on the market and showed it in Paris first. I have fond memories of visiting Aunt Sibyl – as just about everyone did – and I have been fond of the picture since I was a little girl."

"So why didn't you just keep it?" I asked.

"Because I couldn't afford it," she said. "By that time, even as an unknown Polish painting, it was worth more than I could afford.

"There's no way of knowing what our great-grandfather thought he bought; he might not have known, or even been interested. No attributions, or stories about its purchase have come through the family," she said. "He was a self-made man and seems to have had a good eye. He liked it, and thought it would make a lasting reminder of his time in Poland."

"I once asked Mrs Trevelyan just such questions," I said. "She told me she never remembered it not being in the house."

"That doesn't surprise me," Sally said, "but it moves the date of its purchase back even further."

"When did they move to Poland?" I asked.

Sally shrugged.

"No one seems to remember. I had thought it was the early 1900s, but it could have been earlier," she said. "As you may remember, they came back in the mid- or late 1920s."

"So the painting hangs in the family house, but it then goes to Mrs Trevelyan," I said, "where it hung until the mid-1980s."

Sally nodded.

"Yes. My grandmother, Lady Monica, was older than Aunt Sibyl, but Aunt Sibyl married first. Their father died not long after that. Aunt Sibyl and Uncle Edward had houses, and Monica was yet to marry, but had a small flat in London," Sally said. "So, much of the Michelsson furniture went to Sibyl and Edward, including 'Gossip.'

"When Monica married, Grandfather Lipton was enjoying acquiring things for himself, and Monica was an eager buyer, too. I know he liked 'Gossip', as he used to look at it when visiting, but I never heard him discuss it with anyone," she continued.

"I'd studied art and art history, and over the years had taken a close look at all the paintings in the family. When it fell to me to sell the pictures, I had them looked at by several auction houses and if something had attracted attention, I had a specialist look at it," she said. "Everything was in order apart from 'Gossip.' No one was happy with the idea that this rather nice – and saleable – picture had no attribution. When more than one person said it reminded them of a Bérnaud, I stopped showing it around."

There was no arguing that it looked like a French painting. Even I had taken it for one when I first saw it.

"Did you ever think it was?"

She looked down.

"No."

"You can't just show up with a picture by a famous artist," she said. "As a British family in Poland, they couldn't claim it had been in the family for fifty years, and whoever sold it to them probably needed to get rid of it."

"Did your grandfather or Mrs Trevelyan know what it was?" I asked.

"Who knows what my great-grandfather knew?" she said. "He wouldn't have paid a Bérnaud price for it though, even then. Judging by their other stuff, one or two hundred pounds would have been the most he would have paid, which was a lot in those days."

I sat there like a dummy, not knowing what to say or do next.

"I suppose I threw a spanner in the works," I said eventually.

"We had a nearly-good way of moving it on," Sally said.

She reached for her drink and downed about a third of it.

"Don't worry, darling, if it weren't you, someone else – possibly more knowledgeable and less sympathetic – might have spotted it," she said with less concern than I had expected. "Actually, you knew quite enough."

"Does 'Gossip' have provenance?" I asked.

"Nothing. I tried a few times to see who might have

been dealing in Warsaw at the turn of the century, but there wasn't much of Poland left after World War II," she said sadly.

I thought about this. I believed what she had said, but I still believed she was hiding a good deal.

"Sally, it's been good to see you and Arabella, but I think this is where I say good-bye and go back to work," I said. "I don't know enough to cause trouble, and I wouldn't anyway."

"For old time's sake?"

"Call it that," I said.

I reached for my briefcase and coat.

"No!" she exclaimed, and several heads turned towards us.

"Please," she said softly. "Stay."

I was standing, looking down at her.

"If I do, you're going to have to tell me everything – and you have no reason to do that," I said. "And, I'm not sure I want to know."

She continued to stare at me, unblinking, saying nothing.

I sat down.

"Thank you," she whispered.

She reached for her glass, but I took her hand and held it. She didn't resist, but stared at the floor in silence. I let go of her hand, but she took mine as soon as I released her and turned to face me.

"All right, I'll tell you the whole story, but let's go out."

I paid for the drinks and we walked down Piccadilly to Green Park. Sally hadn't said a word since leaving the Keeper's House.

There was a bench in a pool of sunlight and we sat.

I waited for her to continue.

"You do stupid things when you're young and in love," she began. "At least I did."

She thought a minute.

"I don't suppose you can think less of me than you already do," she said. "When I met Jean-Claude, he was just starting Galèries Concorde. It was fun and exciting. We went to artists' studios, junk shops, and all sorts of places looking for things to sell. We were buying cheap modern painters and placing them for sale in bistros, restaurants and the odd small hotel.

"They were modestly priced, and tourists would buy them. The bistro owners would get a commission, and we'd replace the picture that was sold with a new one."

"It sounds exhausting," I said.

"It was, but it was such fun, we didn't mind. It was a good time. Remarkably quickly, we were able to afford better pictures; older ones – but still with no great value. These, with a bit of work on the frames, we were able to place in better restaurants and hotels and make some real money. Enough to rent a very small gallery.

"Buying and delivering the pictures was tiring, and once, I was jostled and put my elbow through a canvas I had just bought. Jean-Claude found someone to repair it, and we began to make contacts in the restoration world. There's a lot of talent out there that finds it very difficult to get work," she said.

Not long after we opened our first Galéries Concorde – the name was always plural – Jean-Claude and I were married. Then, a few months later, Aunt Sibyl died, and her pictures came to me to sell, and that helped give the business a push, but it's also when things went off the rails."

"How many pictures were there?" I asked.

"You probably remember most of them," she said. "She had a few old etchings – she loved old flower pictures. She and her husband recognised quality. We got about half a dozen of them; there were more, but I think she gave a number away.

"Then there were eight oil paintings. Several had come from her husband's family and were of the dead animal variety. There was one good horse picture that we sold almost as soon as we unpacked it," she explained. "Then there were the two Polish ones."

While "Gossip" hung in the front hallway, the other notable Polish picture was in Mrs Trevelyan's bedroom, and I'd only seen it once or twice when moving furniture for her.

"A girl in a field, wasn't it?"

Sally smiled.

"Good memory!" she said. "Yes, it was. We gave it the title 'Wandering,' as she had a rather dreamy quality about her."

"It was on the fantasy-romantic side," I agreed.

"That sold quickly, too," Sally said. "'Gossip' was something altogether different. While in the domestic vein, it had real gravitas, and Jean-Claude came up with the idea of putting it aside and inventing a back-story for it.

"At that time, I didn't know he was going to try to pass it off as a Bérnaud," she said.

Her manner had become more serious, and the memory made her uncomfortable.

"I was pleased to have the picture around; I didn't want to part with it, but Jean-Claude said it could be our fortune, never mind that it didn't belong to us," she said. "When it had hung in our country house for ten years, Jean-Claude took the picture to one of our restorers for a proper look at the paint, canvas, stretcher, and so forth. This restorer was also a talented copyist – "

"And forger?"

Sally nodded.

"Jean-Claude had the idea of putting fake gallery and auction house marks on the back of it."

"To create a provenance," I said.

"That was the clever part," Sally said with a conspiratorial smile. "The idea was to create something that others would interpret – or mis-interpret. None of the labels or marks were forgeries, *per se*. They were more like red-herrings. The name of a stretcher maker, and a partial address might point to Bérnaud, but the inferences would be down to the 'experts.'"

"That is very devious," I said. "If wrong inferences were made, it would be the expert who was the fool and an unwitting conspirator."

She smiled.

"Why Bérnaud?"

"He's known for his Paris café and society paintings, but he's not a name particularly known to the general public," she said, "and several people had mentioned him."

This was true, for after having first seen it, I looked him up before returning to the gallery.

"Forgers tend to go for the big names and big prices," Sally said. "Lesser-known artists aren't forged as often, and, of course, there are fewer experts."

I shook my head in reluctant appreciation.

"It was ingenious. There was nothing that could definitively prove that it was real and nothing to prove it was fake," she said. "While 'Gossip' was at the restorer's *atelier*, I had the idea of having a secret copy made; identical down to the frame and false labels, numbers and chalk marks on the back. When it was done, I couldn't tell it from the original. I still can't."

She laughed.

"That's another of the great bluffs of the art world: recognising the real thing isn't as easy as the television experts would have you believe. 'Experts' will argue forever over the authenticity of something. Ultimately, one will swallow his opinion in the hopes that the rival will reciprocate at an appropriate time.

"Anyway, the restorer, who knew that the painting had come from Poland had the idea to glue a label to the stretcher with 'After Gierymski?' written on it. You should see the back of the pictures; they're wonderful, everything looks authentic, even the rubbing on the chalk-marks. For that label he used an ink of the right composition and a steel nib to write it."

"Who was Gierymski?" I asked.

"Another crafty ruse. There were two Gierymskis. Brothers, Maksymilian and Aleksander. Both painters who lived in the second half of the nineteenth century. Aleksander worked and studied all over Europe: Germany, France, Italy, and in Poland, too. He eventually moved to Italy where he died. Though not typical of their subject matter, you can imagine either of them painting 'Gossip'," Sally said, then laughed. "Wouldn't it be funny if he really did?!"

I could see how easy it would be to get sucked into

such a fraudulent enterprise.

"Is an exact copy of a painting you own a forgery?" I asked rhetorically.

"It's a *copy*," Sally replied definitively. "At least, it's a copy until it's offered for sale. Then, if it's represented as anything except a late twentieth-century work, it would be fraudulent and regarded as a forgery.

"I had to keep my copy hidden from Jean-Claude, but they were both in our little country house and collected lots of dust, smoke, French country dirt, and pollen."

I suppose I secretly hoped that Jean-Claude would change his mind and decide not to sell it at all, but I was wrong. To him, art was just a way of making money, and for him, it was a very easy way."

"What did you plan on doing with yours?"

She made a gesture and dropped her hands in her lap.

"I don't really know. Originally, I wanted it just to keep, but after the bitterness of our divorce and all the fighting that went with it, I have to say, the attachment diminished," she said. "If someone came to the conclusion it was a Bérnaud, then I liked the idea of owning what people believed was a Bérnaud."

I'm sure my mouth was open in disbelief.

"Gob-smacked?" she said. "I'm not proud of myself, but no real harm's been done."

"How old is the copy?" I asked.

"About fifteen years," she said.

"Fifteen years?" I thought. Not long after Mrs Trevelyan died.

"I thought that was smart," she said with a guilty smile. "The copyist is now dead; the painting has an impressive amount of real dirt on it, and the market has inflated."

I shook my head.

"So which one did I see in Bond Street?"

"I don't know."

"Bloody hell, woman! Is this completely out of control?" I exclaimed.

"Jean-Claude is still the major owner of Galèries Concorde. Francesca brought the picture over from Paris a few weeks ago, but I don't know which one."

"How do you not know which one?" I demanded. "Did he find the second one?"

Sally nodded. She had the look of a schoolgirl who had been caught doing something she rather enjoyed doing.

"He came unexpectedly to my apartment after we'd divorced, and saw it in my bedroom," she said, not commenting on how he happened to be in there. "I thought he was going to kill me, but he just laughed. Then he grew suddenly serious, and menacing, and demanded to know for certain that the one I had was the copy."

"It was, wasn't it?" I asked.

"Yes, it definitely was," she replied. "I knew it was because up until then I had kept them separate. Quite reasonably, he wanted to see them together to reassure himself. There was a lot of money at stake. Proving a painting's veracity from the period a hundred years ago is one thing; exposing it as a fifteen-year-old fake is something else."

"Were you serious about not being able to tell them apart?"

"I used to be able to," she said. "But today, I'm not certain whether it's the one with or without the certain mark that's the real one."

"So do you know which one Francesca took back to Paris?"

"Neither of them," she said.

"There aren't *three* are there?"

Sally laughed.

"No; just two. One is in my apartment in Paris. The other is in my hotel room here in London."

"I thought Francesca took it back to France," I said.

"I got to the gallery first."

"So which one do you have?"

"I've got both, but I don't know which is which anymore. It's rather fun not knowing," she giggled. "Oh, don't look so disapproving, darling. Nothing's happened.

I have one alleged Bérnaud and one copy. No one has bought or sold it for a hundred years, or more. Anyway, one of them can be tested."

"But you were trying to sell a *Bérnaud*," I reminded her.

"Well, yes, but that was Jean-Paul and his stupid sister's fault," she said.

"So, what now?"

Sally stood up.

"Tea!"

ଌ

We walked back to Piccadilly in the fading light to an old-fashioned tea shop where we found a table towards the back. There was noise from the serving area, but it inhibited us being overheard. It was nearly full, but we were served quickly.

"You're going to make me be serious, aren't you?" she said.

"You may as well finish," I said. "You were telling me about Francesca."

Sally raised an eyebrow.

"Francesca is a piece of work, isn't she? I should have realised her brother couldn't have been as different as he seemed to be," she said. "She's known about the Bérnaud and the copy for about five years and has been chomping at the bit to get it sold. It's why I'm here; I didn't know she'd brought it to England. I was going to tell her to bring it back until Arabella called and said she'd heard from you."

"But you decided to collect it yourself," I said "So, what happens now? Presumably Jean-Claude isn't going to take the theft of a Bérnaud lying down."

"But it's not a Bérnaud," she said with her smile. "He can't report it missing without any provenance."

"He's not going to be pleased with you!"

"Well, technically, it's not his anyway, it still belongs to Aunt Sibyl's heirs, and Jean-Claude isn't pleased with me anyway. I've just taken a *very* long time to sell it. I may have to remind Jean-Claude of that fact."

"And everyone else has conveniently forgotten about it," I said.

"Arabella knows," Sally said. "Arabella knows *everything*. However, she still has a rather nice Georgian cellaret.

"I suppose I get the picture looked at and see what I can learn."

"There's no chance that it's a real Bérnaud?"

"Who knows? The copyist said it was a first-class picture," she replied. "According to him, Bérnaud is fairly easy to copy *convincingly*. He thought it was quite funny for the painting to be thought of as Polish. He was fairly certain it was French – as did just about everyone we showed it to."

Sally poured more hot water into the tea pot, waited

a few moments and poured us another cup. She settled back and relaxed.

"It is good to see you," Sally said. "I spoilt it, didn't I, all those years ago?"

"One of us would have eventually," I said.

"Would we?" she mused. "Pity."

"You know what the real pity is?" I said. "That the picture hasn't been hanging where people can enjoy seeing it every day. Instead, it's become a piece in some silly game."

We finished our tea and went out into the early evening darkness. Sally held my arm as we crossed Piccadilly and headed to the Underground station. We stopped near the top of the stairs.

"It was good to see you, Gregory," she repeated, and kissed my cheek. "Try not to think too badly of me."

捣

Life got back to normal. Work was busy, and my business partner and I had started interviewing for additional staff. I was in and out of the office visiting customers in the UK and trying to attract new ones.

About a week after seeing Sally, I had an email from Brogan. "Just to let you know that I decided to leave Galèries Concorde and am working in a gallery in Dublin that deals only with living artists. Drop in if you're ever in Ireland."

I emailed him back to congratulate him and wish

him luck, and closed the book on 'Gossip.'

There was no follow up from Sally or Arabella. On a subsequent visit to London, I walked up Bond Street. Galèries Concorde was still there with a large Buffet in the window. Not my favourite, so I didn't stop to look closely, but I did see the stick-insect at her desk.

Several months later, when I returned from a trip, there was a large box on my desk. It was quite deep, but not particularly heavy. It had a courier's label on it, but no return address. I had a morning full of emails, calls and meetings, so it wasn't until lunchtime that I put the parcel on my desk and picked up my letter knife.

Encased in bubble-wrap, I lifted 'Gossip' from the box. I unwrapped it, and there it was, just as I had remembered it. There was an envelope with my name on it, and a short note inside.

If this is a silly game, it's your move. We both know what this is. Appreciate it for what it is. I am sure that Aunt Sibyl would be pleased to know that you have it. One day, we'll have to meet again to establish which of us has the real one.

Love,
Sally
x

Thoughts and Whispers

Hatteras

Thoughts and Whispers

Hatteras

Spring 1973

I do not think I will see Rick Bower again. I met Rick at college. We had many things in common and kept thick company for much of the time we were there. Rick was a philosophy major but had interests which ranged from tennis to Shakespeare. I was studying journalism and taking as many literature courses as my timetable would allow. Rick and I used to bewilder our professors by offering absurd criticisms and throwing well-aimed darts at the topic under consideration. Rick was a brilliant student; I was not. Yet, I felt that I was enjoying being at the university more than he was.

During our junior and senior years, we saw less of each other, but remained good friends. I continued in the way I had for the initial years – working for the newspaper, writing for the magazine and doing odd work with the drama group. Rick abandoned many of his former activities and took up political and social activism. Do the initials SDS mean anything to anyone anymore?

It has been said that the philosophy majors were

usually the first ones to join any liberal movement, and Rick was the first of the philosophers. He was in charge of numerous activities on the campus. He was a McCarthy supporter; an Earth Day coordinator and an untiring worker for the Moratorium. When the students were shot at Kent State, it was Rick who threw the door of my room open and said, "They've *shot* them! My God, they shot – *shot* – them!" with tears running down his face. All great events of the closing years of the sixties; now, only remembered on significant anniversaries.

“”

After leaving college, I got a job writing for a small newspaper and spent my days counting words and picas and my nights trying to relieve eye-strain.

Rick had never been much of a correspondent, but I would hear from him once or twice a year. Usually it was a short note giving a new address and saying that I must come to visit him. The most recent address was for a post box out on Cape Hatteras in Nags Head. The note explained that he was between jobs and living between villages on the Outer Banks. The customary invitation to visit was still on the card. For the first time, I gave serious consideration to taking him up on his offer. I hadn't had a vacation since starting at the paper and I sounded out my boss. He agreed to let me have two weeks off in April. I wrote

Rick and asked if I might come. He replied quickly and told me I could, and should, spend the entire time there.

It was warm when I left my apartment. I headed south figuring my arrival time to be shortly before dinner, if I didn't get lost.

Since I had last seen Rick, he hadn't seemed to do much. He wrote some poetry; he painted a little and had worked as a folk singer in one of the last coffee houses on the East Coast. I couldn't imagine what he had found to do on Cape Hatteras. Perhaps he was selling bait to fishermen. I had been warned that the island was dry, so I made a point of stopping at an ABC store and getting a fifth of gin and some whisky before crossing the sound.

The sun had set by the time I descended the slope of the bridge and arrived on Hatteras Island. The world was still a little orange around the edges, but a thick cloud cover was on the rest of the sky. There was no one at the Nags Head post office, but I asked at an old gas station.

"Bower lives about ten miles north of here. Stay on this road. You'll come to a village called Duck, then the road turns to dirt and sand. Stay on the road and just before it comes to a cyclone fence and goes into soft sand, there's an ark of a house. Rick lives there. Is he expecting you?"

I followed the directions. If Duck was out of the mainstream of civilization, beyond it was absolutely nowhere. Areas had been marked off by an ambitious developer, but nothing had been built. Not really believing the desolation, I stopped my car and got out. The island was about half a mile wide at this point and low clucking sounds came from the land side. I later learned that wild swans, snow geese and other waterfowl were in great numbers on the island.

Several miles farther on, a high pitched roof poked up from the flat sand. Because of the darkness, I couldn't make out the details, but the house was large and old; the sort of beach house that was built at the turn of the century. I pulled into the driveway and as I got out of the car, a figure came from the house and approached me.

"Rick said you'd be here. I didn't think you'd find it."

I introduced myself.

"I'm Carolyn."

I followed her into the house.

"Welcome to Rye."

Inside, the old house was open and had very high ceilings. There was a balcony running across all four walls and a wooden spiral staircase leading up to it. There was a kitchen on the ground floor, separated from the large room only by a bar-like counter.

"Make yourself at home. I don't expect Rick will be

back much before three a.m. He told me to give you anything you wanted." She smiled. "Anything."

"I would like," I began with as little emotion in my voice as possible, "a gin and tonic."

"I don't think we have – "

"In the bag," I said.

Carolyn went to the kitchen and returned with the worst gin and tonic I have ever had. I thanked her. I told her to help herself to the gin.

"Thank you, but I don't drink."

"At all?"

"At all."

We chatted. Carolyn asked about my drive down, but was more interested in hearing about Rick and our time at college. After a while, she stood and went outside. I finished my drink and put my feet up. The next thing I knew, I heard Rick's voice in the kitchen. I'd only been dozing a few minutes, but hadn't heard his car. I went to the kitchen to meet him.

"Well, you finally got down here," he said, shaking my hand and slapping my back.

"It's been a long time since I've had sand in my shoes," I said.

As Rick cooked a quick supper, we talked of college days and old friends. Carolyn did a few odd things to help, but most of them were either done wrong or incomplete. (She set knives, but no forks; only put pepper on the table; and two glasses.)

After supper, when Rick and I had exhausted the accounts of what everyone was doing, I asked him what he did to pay the rent.

"Not a lot. I really don't need much to live on and I still have some family money. I paint and write a little poetry. I'll show you some of the stuff. The poems have gotten me nearly five hundred dollars in the last year. That's about a dollar a poem."

I smiled, but Carolyn burst into gales of laughter, almost shrieking. Rick glanced at her and she lapsed into a quiet giggle, then stopped.

"Did you finish your business early?" I asked.

"What?"

"Carolyn told me she didn't expect you until about three."

"What did you say that for?" he asked her.

"Because that's what you told me."

"No, I didn't. I told you I'd be back around eight-thirty, and I was."

"You said THREE!" she screamed.

"Go to bed," he said, firmly, but not angrily.

"It's only nine-thirty," she whined, softly, then added, "Are you coming up?"

Her voice was almost childish.

"Not yet. Go."

She got up and as she walked past me, she put her

hand on my cheek and said, "See you later alligator."

Rick watched her climb the stairs and cross the balcony to a room. She went in and the door shut.

"I'm sorry I wasn't here to meet you. I expect she made you an awful drink," he said, observing the empty glass on the table.

"Yes. I bought some booze. I thought we could celebrate on a bottle."

"Great. What are we celebrating?"

"My first vacation in two-and-a-half years."

He got glasses while I opened the bottle. Pouring, he said: "May it be peaceful and uneventful."

"Amen."

We talked until two-thirty when I went up to my room under the eaves. I could see the moon over the water and hear the rolling of the waves. Partially drunk and very tired, I was extremely susceptible to the lull of the sea.

When I woke the next morning, tears of rain were rolling down the glass in the window. The drone on the roof was complemented by the soft gurgle in the gutters. Sitting up in bed, I could see the ocean with its turbulence, but had to imagine the surf on the beach, as a soggy sand dune rose between us.

I must have gazed at the ocean for twenty minutes. When I went downstairs, Carolyn was curled in a chair before the fireplace, as fascinated with the fire as I had been with the sea. I sat on the couch where I could watch both the fire and her. She was about twenty-three, attractive, with long, light brown hair. Her pale skin was remarkably smooth and unblemished and she had very long fingers. When she rose from the chair and offered to fix me breakfast, I could see that she wasn't actually tall, but because of her slenderness, she appeared taller than she was. She must have seen me staring, as she batted her eyes at me in an exaggerated manner.

She brought the makings of breakfast which I assembled.

"Is there more coffee?" I called to her, but the only sound which came in return was that of the rain on the back porch.

I walked to the kitchen door and caught a glimpse of her as she disappeared over the crest of a dune and onto the beach. When she returned half an hour later, soaking wet, I had finished eating and was reading by the fire with a fresh cup of coffee. She sat down near me and stared into the fire.

"You ought to change," I said. "You must be frozen."

After a moment, she looked up blankly, but said nothing further.

"You really ought to change your clothes."

"But I like the feel of the clothes sticking to my skin," she said. "It makes me feel like I am being touched."

She continued to stare at the flames, and I continued to read. When I finished the article, I wandered around the room, examining the various objects which were on the tables and shelves.

There was nothing out of the ordinary, just the usual collection of shells, driftwood and odd bits of beach house flotsam. The only things of note were some brass navigational instruments; a sextant, a compass and an old chronometer which did not work. The furniture was neither old nor new. On the wall away from the ocean was a bookcase with more curios from the beach along with several rows of books. There were paperback Perry Masons and Agatha Christies. There were World War II novels, *The Hour Before the Dawn*, *The Naked and the Dead*; there were older books by Dos Passos, Hemingway and Fitzgerald. I took down a copy of *The Sun Also Rises* and opened it. The bookplate looked like a label off a bottle of whiskey as it bore the name Myles Newman and below it, in capital Roman letters, the word "RYE."

"He was a boot-legger – well, a rum runner, actually," Carloyn said from behind me. "I bet he thought it was wonderfully clever naming the house Rye, too."

She smiled in a wistful sort of way.

"Is that what this place was originally?"

She crooked her finger and led the way up the spiral staircase to the balcony, then across to the farthest end where a wooden ladder led to a trap door in the ceiling.

"Don't get too excited," she said. "It's nothing spectacular."

She climbed up, pushed the door open and disappeared. I followed. The attic was nothing spectacular. It was small because the main room of the house went right up to the roof. No one would suspect that there was anything more than bedrooms upstairs. Most prohibition stashes were underground. The only clue was a heavy iron hook on a beam above the gallery where a pulley would have facilitated moving barrels or cases.

The roof sloped sharply, but there was a great deal of space over the bedrooms, which gave the impression of being directly under the roof.

The floor was reinforced to accommodate the weight of a trove of hooch. There was a crawl-space of additional storage which extended nearly the full perimeter of the house. On the inside walls of these rooms were shelves for cases and racks for bottles.

"Did Newman make any of his own booze?"

"I don't think he made anything himself," she answered vaguely. "He was strictly an importer. Ships would anchor about a mile off shore and they brought it in, or Newman would go out to collect it. Apparently there was quite a bit of that sort of thing around here then. This is such a wonderfully desolate house."

Indeed.

We left the attic and returned to the living room. Carolyn's clothes were now dry, but she had done nothing to erase her smeared make-up or comb out the tangles of her damp hair. I asked when she expected Rick back and she said mid-afternoon.

I left her in the house and walked to the beach. It had stopped raining and I looked down the longest and broadest expanse of totally uninhabited beach I had ever seen. A recollection of *Outermost House* came to mind as I looked back at the large frame relic of Rye.

The damp sand clung to my feet and fell off in odd-shaped clumps with every few steps. The dune grasses were the yellow-green which one usually associates with spring, and the waters of the sound, visible across the road, were luxuriant blue despite the dismal day.

I sat on the sand and watched the ocean roll toward me. I was relishing being on the beach and away from work. The honking of wild swans behind me; the soft damp sand and the smell of freshness and salt air were the only impressions which played on my senses.

I sat on the damp sand for an hour.

When I returned to Rye, I didn't see Carolyn. I

went to the kitchen to heat water for more coffee. Reclaiming the place before the fire, I set to rereading Hemingway. About half an hour later, there was the sound of an automobile in the drive. I went out and helped Rick bring in the weekly shopping.

"What sort of opiate is in this place?" I asked.

Rick turned to me slowly.

"What sort of opiate is this place? I got up after ten and nearly fell asleep after a short walk on the beach. I haven't felt so relaxed in ages."

"The ocean has that effect on people, doesn't it?" he said with a laugh. "Did Carolyn cook breakfast for you?"

"Yes," I lied.

"Good."

When the groceries had been brought into the kitchen, Rick and I went to sit down and found Carolyn in the living room.

"She always shows up after the work is done," Rick said as he went to her and kissed her forehead.

"I'm too beautiful to work," she said in a dead-pan fashion which I couldn't read.

"That's right, darling," Rick said.

Rick returned to the kitchen and the opening and closing of cupboard doors, drawers and the rustle of paper described the manner in which he put the shopping away. When he returned, he carried a yellow wrapping paper, damp with a fishy smell. He unwrapped and held up three salt mullets.

"Do you want them for dinner or shall we chop it into bait?"

It was the sort of question, asked in the sort of way, that I had been used to hearing from Rick in college days.

"The blues are running well down at the light and should be along here, too."

I put on a sweater and windbreaker then selected a fishing rod.

"You can imagine how horribly bad I am at this sort of thing," I said as we rose over the wall of dunes separating the house from the sea.

"Don't worry. I haven't done much of it either. You'd think that living here I would fish, swim in the summer and surf, but, no; that's the sort of stuff which always gets put off. Carolyn doesn't like the cape much. I think she hates the ocean. She'd much rather be in a large city. Still, she stays, and I'm glad."

Rick told me he had met her several months before at one of the small cafés he sang in. They had sung together for a while, but when it shut for the season, she had stayed at Rye with him. I couldn't gather if they had done any work since and tried to curb my newspaper inquisitiveness. It took me about fifteen minutes to figure out how my reel worked. My first cast went about a hundred feet, but behind me into the sand rather into the rolling tide.

Eventually, I got the hang of it and made a few respectable casts. I had taken my shoes and socks off and rolled my jeans to my knees. The water was cold, but the feeling of freshness was exhilarating and brought back a touch of the excitement of the seashore not experienced since childhood.

After half an hour of repeated casts without luck, I began to think that the only fish we'd take back to Rye was the one left in the damp yellow paper. In a few moments, the tide would be heading out again and we would have missed our best chance.

There was a jab at Rick's line. He gave a quick jerk and began to reel in.

"I hope it's not a goddam shark," he said disgustedly. As he continued to reel in, he muttered, "It usually is. I get out here about once a month and always catch a damn shark or a sonofabitch ray."

His rod arced toward the white edge of the waves and he backed slowly up the beach. I was busy watching his unique technique when the rod in my hand gave a shock which so startled me that I nearly dropped it and came close to falling the surf. I struggled to gain control, for I feared that the monster I had at the end of my line would certainly break it.

I gave a tug, attempting to set the hook – a move

which had never worked for me before. I regularly ended up falling backwards, or if not that, pulling out some non-vital organ from the fish.

This time, it seemed to work, for the leviathan was still there. I backed up the beach and as I neared Rick, it crossed my mind that our lines were tangled and that we were pulling against each other. Then, Rick's fish appeared in the foam. It was a blue and looked to be about twelve pounds. He walked to the water's edge and lifted the flapping fish up and lay it on a plank of wood.

"Well, there's dinner," he said. "Unless you can come up with something better."

By this time, I felt I had reeled in about five miles of line with still no indication of what was hooked on the end.

"What does it feel like?" Rick asked.

"No idea," I said, feeling that I would be hauled out to sea at any moment.

I reeled in more rapidly and then caught the first glimpse of my catch. It was another blue, and was thrashing in the breaking waves.

It was bigger than Rick's, so he immediately lost interest in watching me land it.

"Get it in before the sharks get it," he said with a laugh.

That was unlikely, so I continued to let it fight.

Rick picked up his fish and walked back to the house.

The blue was in the surf now, and still struggling. It was still possible for it to break free. I waded in and drew it into the shallows and picked it up. I managed to get the hook out once I was far enough away from the water so I wouldn't lose it. One fish would be enough for dinner; Rick would freeze the other one.

I gathered my things and headed back to the house.

"Where's Carolyn?" I asked, taking my fish into the kitchen.

"She's across the road digging clams in the sound. Maybe that's more your speed," Rick said. "Finish your drink and pick up a clam fork and bucket out by the car."

"I'll clean this first," I said. "We can cook it or freeze it."

I didn't hurry. Clams, unlike fish, wouldn't go anywhere. Soon, however, I carried a pail and fork across the road and walked to the edge of the sound. Jeans still rolled, I sloshed into the cold water. It was very clear and ripples in the sand stood out distinctly. I walked slowly along the edge of the bank and, seeing a stream of bubbles, thrust the fork into the sand and pulled upwards.

I picked a good sized clam from the small pile of

sand and dropped it in my bucket. I could see Carolyn several hundred yards from me. She seemed pre-occupied and didn't notice me. I collected more clams in a short strip and several sand crabs which left their tread-like tracks and hurried down into the sand.

My bucket was half full when I reached Carolyn.

She was wearing a long white cotton dress, the sort that was popular when we were in college, but never since. She sat in the damp sand with her feet under her. The lapping water tugged gently on a piece of her dress which floated in the ripples. Her hair hung down the sides of her face and strands stuck to her cheeks with tears. Her eyes were focused on the horizon.

"Carolyn?"

She didn't turn, but spoke softly.

"Have you ever heard anything so sad?"

"So sad as what?" I asked.

"Listen. There are a thousand white swans and snow geese feeding out there."

I was silent for a moment, but heard nothing; then, as one's eyes become accustomed to the night and perceive the stars, I began to hear the distant noises of myriad water fowl. They were plaintive, but wouldn't move the average person to tears.

"Oh, God, that's sad."

She sniffed a little and then turned to me.

"Don't take me too seriously. I just can't help

myself. Let's find some more clams."

She picked up a partially filled bucket and walked into the water and randomly dug a few clams.

"This is a beautiful place, isn't it?" she asked. "It's too bad I hate it so much. I used to have a lot of friends. Now, there are only a few business acquaintances who ever come to Rye. You're the first real guest in a year."

"I'm very glad I came."

"I hope you can say that when you leave."

As she spoke, three heron descended from the sky and landed only a hundred yards from us. We were both taken with the beauty of these birds and stood watching them. When they rose and flew away, it was dark. Carolyn took my arm as we waded back to the path and walked to the house.

Rick would cook the fish, and the clams would be steamed, so there was little work to do. I went up to my room to change my trousers. When I came down, I sat by the fire and read Hemingway, until I briefly drifted off. Although I was only out for about fifteen minutes, my sleep was alive with dreams. Fantastic birds spread their all-encompassing white wings and seemed to blot out the daylight. As one flew near my face, great tears fell from the black bead eyes and circles extended outward from where they hit the still water of the sound. Carolyn appeared as Ophelia, floating on her back watching the great flight of birds. A vintage car drove to the water's edge and a man got out, walked up to me and said, "It's so sad," turned and vanished.

It was in a state of semi-confused consciousness that I awoke. Dream and reality had merged and it was several moments before I was fully aware that Carolyn was actually next to me, gently shaking my shoulder.

"Take me away from here," she whispered.

"What?" I mumbled.

"Take me away from here. Help me. Help me!"

"What can I do – ?"

"Carolyn!" Rick called from the kitchen. "Just wake him up; I need you in here."

She took both my hands and looked into my eyes.

"Make him stop!" she whispered.

She rose and left the room.

At dinner, Rick was his usual charming self and we joked and I listened to fishing stories, Outer Banks history and legends, and funny tourist stories. Carolyn remained silent and gave no indication of uneasiness. Midway through dessert, a car rumbled down the road and stopped at the side of the house.

Rick went out to see who it was, and Carolyn stood watching through the window. After a few minutes, Rick came back and the car drove away.

"Someone looking for Kill Devil Hills," Rick said.

"Kill Devil Hills?"

"A town below Kitty Hawk. It's not often that people make the wrong turn, but it does happen. You haven't been down the rest of the island, have you?

"You and Carolyn should go tomorrow. I've got some stuff to take care of anyway, and the rest of the Outer Banks are pretty interesting. Take him all the way to Ocracoke," he said to Carolyn.

She said nothing but sat perfectly still in her chair and stared across the room.

Later, while I was helping Rick clear up, we noticed a strange smell coming from the main room. We looked in and found that Carolyn had set one of her long fingernails on fire and burnt the tip of her finger.

&

In the morning, Carolyn and I began our drive down the coast. We reached Buxton where we had a sandwich and walked around Hatteras Light, but only briefly as we had to catch the ferry to Ocracoke island.

Carolyn was fairly well versed in Outer Banks history and lore, mostly from boredom, she said, and proved to be an interesting guide. We pulled to the side of the road and climbed a small observation platform to look at the wild horses descended from those ship-wrecked over four hundred years ago.

When we arrived at Ocracoke, the village looked deserted. We drove around the claw-like crescent, stopping to look at the large, old frame houses and to walk on the empty wharf near the Coast Guard Station. We wandered around the small British cemetery before stopping for lunch in the restaurant of the only open motel on the island.

At lunch, Carolyn suggested that we drive back up the road and pick a spot to walk on the beach.

It was a sunny day directly overhead, but there was haze on the horizon which threatened to blow inward. There was no problem in finding a strip of deserted beach, as it was all barren. What few people who had come to the island came with the common goal of being alone. We parked by a ramp over the dunes. Carolyn had brought a blanket and we found a soft sheltered hollow of dry sand and stretched out in the warmth of the sun.

I sat watching the ocean while Carolyn went for a walk down the beach. It had turned cooler and the sun was behind the clouds. I walked up the beach towards her. She was coming towards me, scanning the sand, bending over to examine a shell or piece of driftwood; deciding whether to put it in her leather bag to take home or to leave it on the beach to be ground into colored powder.

The tide had begun to recede and I walked on the wet sand leaving clear footprints which would be preserved for twelve hours. Carolyn was aware of the ebbing tide also and scrawled her name and a few lines of free verse on the smooth surface with a broken shell.

"It's about as long as anything I do will last," she said. Her affinity for the ocean was very great; she waded into it and let the water swirl around her knees. My toes were numb from the short walk up the water's edge and I couldn't conceive of walking into the surf the way she did. When we were back at the car, we decided to catch the next ferry back to Hatteras and have dinner. It was already growing dark and patches of fog blew over us as we drove to the north of the island.

The ferry ride was a little rougher than it had been in the morning, but no water came on deck. Carolyn, I feared, could feel the motion as she locked her arms beneath her knees and rested her head on them. I asked if she were all right. She said she would be. Still, she rode in this position until we reached the restaurant of the Atlantic Hotel.

"Are you hungry?" I asked.

"Ravenous," she answered breathily.

We ate our meal, served at great length, and found the world covered in thick fog when we left.

As we made our way north, Carolyn asked what time it was. It was seven o'clock.

"Let's stop at the lighthouse again. It ought to be neat in the fog."

"It will be after nine when we get back to Rye, now," I said.

"Come on. It'll be neat."

There was no one on the road to the light. There was no one in the parking lot, either. I parked the car and looked up at the revolving beacon. Its shafts were like amputated arms, as they only were able to pierce the fog for a few hundred feet and their outline was sharply defined like blades on a giant pin-wheel.

Carolyn got out of the car and walked toward the lighthouse then disappeared into the darkness. I tried to follow. The air, though cooler than the afternoon, was warm for April. I walked up the path to the ruins of the old light house, but didn't see Carolyn. It was difficult enough to see in the fog, but from the flashes of light of the beacon to the total darkness when the light was at right angles reduced visibility to nearly nothing.

I descended the small dune to the beach and walked towards the light.

There was a long wooden jetty reaching into the pounding surf. Carolyn was sitting on it at the water level and waves rolled in and covered all but her head and shoulders. I ran to the jetty and called to her. She didn't answer, but looked towards me for a moment then turned back to the ocean.

"Come back here, you lunatic girl!"

I had no intention of walking out on that algae-covered row of piling and slipping into fifty-degree water.

"Carolyn!"

Finally, she stood and precariously made a turn and began to walk back to the beach.

When she slipped and fell in, I was more angry than fearful for her safety. I ran into the frigid water and unceremoniously dragged her out. It was less than two feet deep but was nearly paralyzing.

After putting her down on the beach, I was about to tell her how incredibly stupid she was, when she sat up and pulled her knees to her and began to moan.

"Help me!" she gasped.

I held her tightly, hoping that two of us shivering together might warm one of us.

"I can't stand it any longer. Take me back to Rye as fast as you can. Rick – I need Rick. Please, help me!"

I dragged her back to the car, put her in the back seat and threw the blanket over her.

We drove into the fog.

About fifteen minutes later, Carolyn sat up and asked me to go faster. The fog held me to a crawl that made her more impatient than ever, and nearly hysterical, but she became subdued as we approached Kitty Hawk.

"What's going on down here?" I asked, impatiently

"Can't you guess."

"I think so. What do you need?"

"Heroin," she said, barely audibly.

"And Rick supplies you?"

"Rick supplies three states. The boat comes in tonight. That's why he wanted you out of the way."

She paused, breathing deeply, her fingers spasmodically grabbing at nothing.

"He figured I could make it longer than I can. He'll probably throw me out now, and I don't know what he'll do to you. Perhaps if you promised never to say anything – "

The road turned to dirt beyond the village of Duck. Rumbling and grinding in the sand, in the fog, with Carolyn wailing in the back seat, is something I shall never forget. We were within five hundred feet of Rye when Carolyn insisted I stop the car.

She jumped out and ran to the top of a dune which commanded a view of the house and the beach. I followed and stood beside her.

Rye was ablaze with light showing through every window, and on the beach, blue and red dome lights flashed as uniformed men surrounded a grounded trawler.

Thoughts and Whispers

Snow on Snow
A Westbury Tale

Thoughts and Whispers

Snow on Snow
A Westbury Tale

U ncle Charles was sitting in the corner of his library. It was about nine in the evening and a snifter of brandy was on the table beside him. The fire burned steadily, but still cast flickering shadows about the room. Some light from the hall came into the library, but the main source was the green-shaded floor lamp near his armchair which illuminated both him and the book in his lap.

"Am I disturbing you?" I asked. "Caroline baked the Christmas cookies today and I left a tin with Julia down in the kitchen."

Uncle Charles smiled and thanked me and told me to be sure to thank Caroline.

"What are you reading?" I asked.

I knew this question could reveal an unexpected diversity. Over the years, he had answered with such things as *Representative Democracy*, *The Jewish War*, *Democracy in America*, *L'Education Sentimental*, *The Education of Henry Adams*, *Notes from the Underground*, *Lolita*, and *The Carpetbaggers*.

Today, it was *The Turn of the Screw*. Most of what Uncle Charles read was unknown to me. I had read a surreptitious copy of *Lolita* while at the Academy, but the rest were just titles that my friends with arts degrees talked about. However, I had read *The Turn of the Screw* for English class, also in high school. My memory was largely based on the movie versions of it.

"I'm afraid I haven't got very far," he said. "I must have read it ten times over the years, and each time I read it, it frightens me more."

My long conversations with Uncle Charles had taught me to wait for him to speak and not prompt or question him until I was certain he wasn't going to pick up his thread.

"I've only read about five paragraphs this evening," he said.

I was going to apologize for interrupting him but checked my impulse. I looked at him, and I thought he appeared pale in the warmth of the incandescent lamp and fire, and his thoughts seem to have drifted off. Although almost eighty, this was not normal for Uncle Charles, whose mind and memory was clear.

It was nearly a full minute before he spoke.

"Do you remember Damian Greene?" he asked.

"The partner at Dexter's?"

Dexter's was one of Westbury's two leading department stores, alas, now both closed.

"That's right," Uncle Charles confirmed. "He also owned 57 Mason Street with another business partner."

Fifty-seven Mason Street was a prime *beaux arts* apartment building built in the early 1920s. There was a mistaken notion that it was designed by McKim, Mead and White, but the truth was that it had been done by an architect who had apprenticed with them. Although it had gone through a period when the style was maligned, the building had always been well-maintained inside and out and had subsequently been the place where Westbury's rich had gone when they downsized.

I had met Mr. Greene at the Westbury Club several times and seen him from my school days in Dexter's. He was a handsome man who was by nature a leader. He had been athletic in high school and during his curtailed college years. He had become an Army captain during the war and according to Uncle Charles, won a chestful of medals for reasons never discussed.

"Were you school friends?" I asked.

"I didn't go to school with everyone," he replied. "He was close to my age, but I didn't know him until the 1960s when we did some business together."

"He died recently, didn't he?" I asked.

"Last week."

There was another pause. I sensed he wanted to tell a story but hadn't decided which part of it to begin with. This, in itself, was unusual, as Uncle Charles's stories were well-honed and well worth listening to. He spoke in anticipation of my next thought.

171

"A week or so before he died, I visited him in his care home," he began. "Now, I've never told anyone this first part – though your mother may have mentioned the parts we all knew – but when I saw Damian, he told me the whole story.

"Back in the 1960s, before Damian and I began working together, I was having dinner with several colleagues at Butler and Frobisher and I saw Damian a few tables away. I knew him, but apart from the odd occasion that I went into Dexter's, our paths didn't often cross.

"What caught my attention was that he was with a little girl who could not have been more than twelve."

I made some expression that was more shock than surprise, and Uncle Charles caught my inflection.

He laughed.

"In those days, the assumption would have been that if this was not a daughter – and Damian was a confirmed bachelor – it would be a niece or goddaughter – not a Nabokovian nymphet, though the film came out around that time."

He thought a moment.

"Which is the better attitude, do you think? To make the supposition of an innocent relationship of a familiar nature, or to assume the depravity of one or the other, or both?" he asked. "At the time, I thought it might be a niece, but even then, I was struck by the sophistication of her clothes. She wore a deep blue velvet dress; her long hair had been carefully brushed and she wore a matching blue velvet hairband. The impression I got was that she was also wearing some makeup. Had she not been wearing white ankle socks and flat patent leather shoes, I might have taken her for being older."

It was my turn to laugh.

"Was the conversation at your table so dull that you had time to notice all this?" I asked.

Uncle Charles, too, was a bachelor, but he had many female friends, though to my knowledge, none as young as twelve. My question did not provoke him, which was another tiny indicator that this story might have more to it than I was anticipating.

"They appeared to have arrived shortly before we did, so I could watch them throughout the meal. The angle of the table enabled me to see most of the girl's face but never make eye contact.

"She struck me as a rather accomplished young lady for her age and she and Damian made more conversation than I would have expected – not that my experience of twelve-year-olds is extensive. She wasn't fully confident, but she managed the meal well and had excellent table manners.

"Damian seemed to be telling her about things, perhaps about the food, how clothes were bought for the store, or his adventures during the war. Who knows? It's not as though he did all the talking, either. She asked questions and seemed to tell him things, too.

"My associates wanted to continue talking over endless cups of coffee, whiskies, brandies, and whatnot, so Damian and the girl had left long before we did."

For the first time, as if reminded by what he had said, he reached for the glass by his side and took the smallest of tastes.

"Do you want something? I think Julia's still downstairs."

I declined, though I took that as a warning that he'd be going on for some time.

"While from time to time I thought about the curious dinner of the greying bachelor and the school girl, there was no opportunity to learn more. I didn't encounter Damian, nor did I see the girl about town. That would have been highly unlikely, anyway.

"It was more than a year later, I was having dinner again at Butler and Frobisher – "

"It was always one of your regular places to eat, wasn't it?"

The venerable restaurant had closed after eighty years in the mid-1980s, leaving dozens of affluent old men wandering the streets looking for a suitable substitute. The Westbury Club rose to the occasion, probably prompted by these men, starving for good food and civilized service, and invested in its kitchens and dining rooms.

"I'm glad you had the chance to eat there," he said, reflecting. "As I said, about a year-and-a-half later, I was there again, this time with the Porters and your parents. I think we were celebrating your mother's birthday. Her actual birthday had been the week before and I had been to a party at your house, but the Porters had missed it, and because your father, Bill Porter and I had been working on a project, I joined them.

"It was your mother who made the first sighting and observation. 'Look Charles, isn't that Damian Greene?' she asked me. I was sitting next to her, so my line of sight was almost exactly like hers. 'Whose the young girl with him?'

"And there they were again. They were at the same table, and while Damian looked essentially the same, the girl was taller and more sophisticated. Her hair was still long with bits pulled back and pinned at the back of her head, and she wore what your mother called an 'LBD' more suitable for cocktail parties. She said it was 'age appropriate' but expressed surprise that she was wearing nylons and heels that she said were *not* age-appropriate."

I chuckled as my mother's sense of propriety – like most of my family's – was about fifty years out of date, and my cousins and I grew up with some pretty old-fashioned notions. The fact that such things were not unfamiliar to Uncle Charles also amused me.

"I couldn't see them as well as your mother, and she appeared as fascinated with the two of them as I had been the first time I'd seen them, and kept glancing towards them.

"'There's something going on there,' she whispered to me, half way through the meal. 'I don't mean Damian Greene, I mean *her*. She's working on something.' I asked if she thought she was trying to seduce him. She thought a moment, 'She could give that a good shot,' she said, 'but this is something else. Something more serious.'

"Your mother remained fixed on the two, and her contribution to the table's conversation was much less than usual. Eventually, they left, and your mother watched them closely. As they went out, Damian glanced at our table, nodded and raised his hand in a wave, but the girl's and your mother's eyes connected, and remained so until Damian spoke to her to lead her out.

"We were at the restaurant for more than half an hour longer and our laughter grew louder, but your mother said almost nothing."

The log in the fire broke on cue, sending sparks up the chimney, confirming that this was not going to be like Uncle Charles' usual stories. The involvement of my mother added an unexpected dimension to these incidents as her no-nonsense practicality was as strong as Uncle Charles'. Had she thought that Damian Greene was doing anything wrong with the girl, she wouldn't have let him leave the restaurant with her.

Uncle Charles fussed with the log in the grate, reassembling the pieces and placing another log on top. It crackled, and the smell of a different wood wafted into the room as he put the screen back.

Once settled in his chair again, he took another tiny sip of his drink and picked up his story.

"Your mother came to see me the next morning. She called me during breakfast, and I arranged to meet her at the coffeeshop that used to be down the road from the club."

"Benson's" I said.

He nodded.

"I got there first and had ordered a coffee which I was drinking when she arrived. I didn't know what she wanted to talk to me about; I had feared it was something to do with your father.

"She quickly settled herself when she arrived and waited impatiently for the waitress, not speaking. I tried a few pleasantries, saying that the meal the night before had been good; that the Porters were on good form, and that it had been nice to extend her birthday like that, but my efforts only received monosyllabic answers.

When the coffee arrived and the waitress departed after asking if she wanted a doughnut or a piece of pie, she fired her first question.

"'How well do you know Damian Greene?' she asked. I said we knew who each other were but that was all, just like I said to you. 'You must warn him,' your mother said next. 'That girl is a danger to him.'

"Her speed and directness and the subject caught me off balance, as I was expecting her to tell me something about Jonathan, or you.

"'What makes you say so, Patricia?' I asked. She took a breath and paused. I think she realized that she needed to sound objective and calm in the matter. 'When you pointed out Mr. Greene and the girl, like you, I thought it was a simple case of having a meal with a daughter or niece. I always thought he looked and acted the perfect gentleman when I've gone to Dexter's. I've never had more than a general conversation with him, but he was always friendly and seemed to remember everything I said.'"

I thought Uncle Charles' memory must be phenomenal, as he caught my mother's phrasing and syntax exactly.

"'What I noticed as I watched them was that she didn't act like a thirteen-year-old. Her manners were too good, and she was comfortable with them. Also, she appeared to be running the conversation, not just talking the way girls do that age. She was focused, and there was none of the adolescent spontaneity that you see in ordinary girls. She's been trained to act this way.' The first question that came to my mind was, 'Why? What was the point?'"

Uncle Charles glanced at the fire.

"Next, your mother looked at it from a different angle: 'Do you know how long it would take to train a child to act like that?' she asked. 'I tried to watch her more closely – it wasn't easy, as I was trying to eat and take part in our conversations, too,' she said. 'I was trying to see if she was actually the age she looked. Perhaps she was eighteen or twenty-one but small and of a slim build, trying to look young. That, at least, opened up some more conventional possibilities, but hardly something Mr. Greene would parade at Butler and Frobisher.'"

Again, I laughed, but this time more in surprise at my mother's astuteness in this seamier side of life. Uncle Charles smiled at my amusement and seemed to understand what had generated my response.

"She concluded that the girl was very young, and that was what had provoked the urgency of her call," Uncle Charles said.

"'When the girl and I looked at each other, I did not see what I expected,' she said. 'I know the looks of little girls,' she continued. 'They can look honestly innocent;

they can look smug; they can look mischievous; they can look cross; they can look what they think is seductive; and they can sulk. This girl, when she looked at me had a look that said, "Don't even think of getting in my way," and it chilled me as it was other-worldly.'"

Mom was a primary and middle school teacher and deputy principal. She knew children well. I was used to her demonstrative statements about difficult children, but they were invariably of the letting-off-steam variety, and I had never heard her talk about a child inspiring fear. Uncle Charles's next comment echoed that.

"Your mother wouldn't intrude into my day and say something like that without good reason, and I was taken aback. I, of course, had never looked the girl in the eye so hadn't sensed anything unusual, certainly not the demoniac element that she implied."

What he said took the matter to a level I hadn't gleaned from my mother's words.

"Did you do anything?" I asked.

My uncle opened his hands.

"What could I do? The best I thought I could do was, the next time I saw him, to say I'd seen him at Butler and Frobisher and ask how he enjoyed his meal. If he felt he needed to say something, that would give him the opportunity."

He took another deep breath and sighed. For some time he said nothing. He eyed his drink but did not touch it.

"I have not told you the whole truth, Stephen," he said finally. "I *did* know Damian Greene before we did business. We served together in the war, and I was present for several of the events that led to his well-deserved decoration."

Uncle Charles never spoke about his war experiences. We knew he'd been in Europe, but he'd never be drawn on where he was or what he did. Whether this was because it was too painful to recall, or too secret, we never knew.

"During our time liberating Europe, we came across people who were lost, abandoned, or hiding," he said. "At that time, we were following the fighting and would gather these people, treat them, feed them, and organize transport for them to temporary camps where they would receive proper attention before returning home or going elsewhere."

"How big a group were you?"

"By then, there must have been about sixty of us – ten officers, fifty men – from different units that had been scattered, lost or left behind for other reasons until areas were secured and the main holding forces followed. It was pretty *ad hoc*, but it seemed to work. One of our buddies was a guy called Sims. He had just become a captain and Damian and I were still first lieutenants. In many ways, the three of us were similar.

None of us were career army, and we found ourselves doing things that were not in our nature – but that was true of millions of others. We did the job and ate and drank well when we could.

"We helped where possible; we played with the children and tried to teach them baseball if there was time; we didn't plunder anything and kept our hands off the women. Again, none of this is remarkable, but the exceptions have got all the publicity. One of the main reasons for not getting too close to anyone was that you never knew who you could trust. We all knew men who had fallen for a pretty face or good figure only to find themselves dead in the morning.

"Then we met Alanna."

ᏺ

As this is Uncle Charles's story, I'm going to let him tell it without my interruptions, which were few.

Late one afternoon about six of us were circling a series of farm buildings looking for the dead, wounded, or hiding, when Damian heard a groan from under a collapsed shed. With guns ready, we advanced, and Ted Sims goes in first and motions for us to follow. It was almost funny as when we went through the doorway, we found it was the only wall standing. We looked about and discovered an arm coming out from under a wooden partition.

I went back to call for some more men, as it would

take more to move it clear without injuring whoever was under it. Ted spoke gently, saying that we were helping. He said this in half a dozen languages and the arm waved in acknowledgement. It was clothed in a rough farmer's jacket and the hand was dirty, so it was impossible to determine whether it was male or female.

While others scoured the area for other survivors, a dozen of us began moving the wooden wall which had come down as a single piece, but was held down by material from the roof. While Ted kept talking, mostly in English, to give reassurance, we cleared all we could without walking on the wall and crushing the person beneath.

It took about twenty minutes before we'd not only cleared the debris on top of the wall but a path to follow and a place to set it down once we had lifted it. With Ted still talking, we each stood by a section and prepared to lift. On command, we lifted it about a foot. It wasn't heavy, but it was unstable and was threatening to break apart. As we lifted, the figure underneath revealed itself to be female with a long, loud scream. Ted dropped to his knees to look underneath and the men on either side of him moved along to take up the weight he had dropped.

We could hear him speaking softly, and he reached in and we heard things moving.

"All right, take it away!" he shouted, putting his head

up.

Once we'd dumped it in a pile, we returned to see the girl.

"My group stay here, the rest of you continue searching. Damian, fetch the medic," he ordered.

The figure moved a little and looked up at Ted and smiled, then put her head down. The jacket had a large dark red stain on it. She had evidently been pierced by a nail in the wall. It had remained in her until we lifted it.

Ted continued with soothing words; he told her help was on the way. I passed him my canteen which he held for her. The medics checked her over on the spot, cutting the bloody jacket off her, putting a pad on the wound, and moving her to open ground on a stretcher. There were no broken bones, the puncture wound looked worse than it was, and apart from dehydration and poor nourishment for who knows how long, she was expected to make a full recovery. During this process, she grasped Ted's hand and held it until the medics loaded the stretcher into the truck. She told him her name was Alanna.

For all the destruction, death and blood we had seen, this living, saving moment of human connection affected us all, and we've carried it with us. Damian and I spoke of it, but Ted was silent. The war ended a few months later and we went back home and became civilians again. I think each soldier coped with peacetime life differently. Most of us remembered the good times, the comradery, the SNAFUs, the idiotic characters we met and the friendships we formed. Others, couldn't escape the horror, and for those still alive, it continues to haunt them.

Damian and I were able to get back into ordinary life without much trouble. We relished the routines that those who hadn't experienced war couldn't comprehend. Ted wasn't from the area. He lived in the middle of Pennsylvania somewhere between Harrisburg and Pittsburgh. Damian had a short letter from Ted about a year after we got home. Damian was already working at Dexter's and my life was well underway, so we were surprised to find that Ted's wasn't. In his letter, he announced that he was headed back to Europe to see if he could find Alanna. Something had touched him that he could not shake, and he needed to get it out of his system.

We thought it was a futile quest but hoped, that whatever the outcome, he'd find his feet and get on with his life.

Our lives continued in the routines we loved, and we'd forgotten about Ted's expedition until about ten months later when we both received invitations to his wedding. He'd even asked Damian to be his best man, as he was the one who had first heard the sounds of Alanna's distress. We went, of course, to support Ted and to meet Alanna properly. We had a brief chance to see them before the wedding. Alanna was lovely in a dark, European way. Damian noted on the way back that anyone who had been to Europe would have thought her beautiful, but that American tastes may not have recognized it. For all her beauty, she had scars on her hands and cheek, but you'd have to look closely to notice. At the wedding, when she was wearing makeup, she looked flawless.

She was learning English which, though strongly accented, was grammatically perfect.

"I knew Ted would come for me," she said, reaching over the table to take his hand. "It never occurred to me that he would not."

That summed it up. She had enchanted him from the beginning and that was it.

From the time he had rediscovered her, Ted focused on restoring her health and her peace of mind. The United States was a different world for her, and under Ted's care, she gradually adjusted.

They settled near Ted's hometown, and we heard from them at Christmas. Ted had a good job as a project manager for a property development company. He would have been ideal for that as a good leader and someone who was hands-on and practical, so we were not surprised to learn that each year that passed he was doing better and better. Alanna had joined community activities working with a number of organizations including fruit producers, the 4H Club and the county fair. Several years after their wedding, the annual letter to accompany the Christmas cards was written by Alanna, not by Ted, which we thought was a very good sign. One or both would add a note to us individually.

We weren't surprised when early in the 1950s they had a daughter. Elizavita was, by all accounts, exceptional – just like everyone else's children.

The routine of work and our Christmas card connection to Ted and Alanna continued. It was ironic that Alanna wrote the notes to us as we had only seen her in Europe when she was semi-conscious, and at her wedding when she was distracted. Memories of the war faded and by the end of the 1950s, I had fallen off Ted and Alanna's Christmas card list. It was fifteen years since I had seen him, so it was hardly surprising. Apart from seeing Damian when I went to Dexter's, or in various restaurants, he and I did little more than exchange pleasantries. Our shared memories weren't ones we cared to revisit often.

It was for those reasons that I never associated the young girl in the restaurant with Elizavita.

I only saw her those two times, a year apart, and for the next twenty-five years, I seldom thought of Ted and his family. As I said, Damian and I had some business from time to time, but we didn't talk about the war.

Damian had seemed to age and although only in his mid-fifties appeared older. His manner was slower than his contemporaries, but he seemed physically healthy and there was nothing wrong with his mind.

A few weeks ago, I visited him in his care home where he had been since having a stroke. It was a beautiful place with lawns, woods, porches and cozy rooms. I thought it an ideal place to spend the last months of one's life without the risk of dying solvent.

Damian's stroke had left him paralyzed on much of the left side, so he was in a wheelchair. It was a bright February day and a recent snowfall had covered the world in snow. It was still new enough that it glistened, and the paths had been cleared; it was possible to push him for a circuit around the grounds.

I was chatting to him, and he would answer from time to time. He had a lot of speech therapy and was able to have a conversation that was not painful for either of us. We were about three quarters of the way around the building, when on rounding a corner, we came on a large section of lawn. There was an expanse of unbroken snow with a drift in the middle that brought to mind the elegant shapes some sculptors strive for. I was struck by the sharp definition between the white of the snow and the blue of the sky and was admiring the scene when Damian suddenly let out a cry and held out his arm and waved in protest.

"No! No!" he shouted, waving at nothing I could see. "Take me back to my room!"

"But what – ?"

"Take me back!"

"Are you all right?" I asked, bending down to look at him.

"Yes, I'm fine, just take me back!"

As we were more than half-way around the building, I pushed him forward, but he protested loudly.

"Not that way, turn around and go back the way we came!"

I had never heard Damian raise his voice. I was startled by his vehemence, not to mention the strength of it.

He said nothing as I pushed him back. I tried to deduce what he had seen that had so upset him. There were no animals there, and the sun was high enough that there was little likelihood of sinister shapes in the shadows. Besides, Damian had shown remarkable courage during the war and was never one to be frightened by sounds or tales that unsettled the rest of us. Before we turned the corner, I glanced back to see if I had missed something, but there was only snow to the edge of the woods.

When we reached his room, a nurse came to help him with his coat and move him from his wheelchair into his comfortable armchair. He had been allowed to bring it along with a few other bits of his furniture.

I went to fetch some hot tea from near the nurses station. When I returned, he seemed less agitated. I put his cup before him on his hospital table and he pulled it towards himself. He then fished down the side of the chair and produced a hip flask from which he poured a healthy shot into his tea before returning it to its hiding place.

"Shh!" he said with a conspiratorial smile.

We drank our tea in companionable silence before I ventured:

"I don't know what you saw, but you gave me a hell of a fright."

I said it with a laugh, but he gave me a warning look.

"I wish to God it was funny, but it's not," he said, his voice a rough whisper.

He leaned, putting his head in his right hand, hiding his face. For a moment I thought he might break down, but he was silent and still.

"I've never known you to be afraid of anything, Damian," I said. "What is it?"

He didn't reply, and I thought he might ignore the comment.

Then, he leaned forward and looked up at me with a bemused expression.

"That's the problem: it's. . . *nothing.*"

He continued to look at me with his quizzical

expression, and I shared his incomprehension, but for different reasons.

He gave a deep sigh and settled back in his chair.

"I'll tell you the story, but I swear, if you laugh, I'll never speak to you again," he said. His voice was stronger and under control now, and he sounded like the Damian I knew.

"I don't have to remind you about Ted and Alanna," he began. "Theirs was one of many extraordinary romances to develop during the war. Theirs survived, at least, I think it did. I lost track of them in the sixties, and even with the coming of the internet, I never tried to track them down.

"You will remember how sick Alanna was when Ted brought her back after the war. She was still recovering, but her problems were less medical than emotional. She was utterly devoted to Ted who she saw as her rescuer. She often said that without him, she would be dead. As you know, Ted returned her love. He had sought her out as soon as travel for civilians became possible again.

"Although it took him some time, he found her with greater ease than might be expected. He had some contacts and a few lucky breaks, but he maintained that he seemed to know where he was going, as if called by Alanna.

"There was endless paperwork – her documents were gone – but he stayed with her until the bureaucrats and the Army had ground through the formalities. Once back in America, she quickly recovered physically. It would take longer to adjust to losing everything and everyone she knew and then adapt to a new way of life. Each one of those things must have been frightening for a young girl, and it took a long time before she began to feel comfortable.

"Ted told me that her biggest fear was that he would suddenly be gone. He reassured her that there was no fear of that, but she never took him for granted. The farm she had lived on was pretty basic and the local shops never had much to sell. The country had been at war for nearly a third of her life, so to come to the United States that hadn't been bombed, over-run, starved and left ruined must have been as strange to her as landing in Oz was to Dorothy."

Damian told this part of the story easily and it evoked fond memories.

"I think Alanna worked very hard. She wanted to please Ted, and he said she wanted to deserve her new life, hence her involvement with the community. I don't know if it was accident or design that caused Ted to settle in a farming area, but it certainly resonated with Alanna who was able to make friends based on common interests and experiences.

"Then Elizavita was born.

"They were overjoyed, of course, and she was a

beautiful child. She was happy, healthy, clever, did well at school and learned to play the piano exceptionally well. She wasn't a prodigy, but she was very accomplished and played with confidence.

"I heard her play when I visited them when she was about eleven. They had a lovely home in an old-fashion house with gables and a porch at the front and an acre or two where they grew vegetables, kept chickens and a goat. It was small scale as Ted had his job, and Alanna her community and social activities. Elizavita was good with the animals.

"A couple of years later, Ted and Alanna wanted to go back to Europe to see if they could trace any of her family. It took a long time to organize the visas as so many countries were virtually inaccessible to Americans. Now an American citizen, it was harder for Alanna to get the visas, but they persisted. When all finally fell into place, they asked me if I would look after Elizavita for two weeks. She had liked me, and the idea of seeing someplace different appealed to her. It was summer, so there was no requirement for her to be at school. For my part, I had hardly ever taken a holiday, so getting time off was possible," Damian said.

"This was the first of two visits. Elizavita was twelve at the time, but she acted as though she'd be twenty on her next birthday. I suppose I had been foolish to think this would be easy. I took her around Westbury and showed her things that I thought she'd be interested in. Along with the historical sites, I took her to the stables where we organized some riding lessons for her later in the week. It was hot, so I took her to the beach at the lake."

It was a hangover from Westbury's nineteenth century paternalism that various lakes dotted on the outskirts of the city had beaches that were for the employees of various major industries and companies. The facilities at these beaches varied by the profitability of the companies that owned them. Some beaches hadn't been improved in decades; others had modern changing rooms, snack bars and a full panoply of beach chairs, floats, life-preservers and slides. Dexter's shared a beach with one of the larger machine shops. Employees paid fifty cents a car for access. It was usually enough to pay for a lifeguard.

"I seldom used the lake, though there were good parties and barbecues there. I'd swim once in a while and take out one of the turnabouts and maybe fish a little. I took Elizavita a few times. She made some friends and didn't do anything too outrageous. One day, she asked if we could go out in a boat. She wasn't happy that I made her wear a life-jacket because it would spoil her even suntan, but when she saw all the others were wearing them, she stopped protesting.

"I took her to the movies with a girlfriend she'd

made at the lake. I knew the girl's mother who worked in the fabric and sewing department and her husband worked in accounts. The two spent time together and had fun. One afternoon when Mrs. Wyman returned Elizavita, she asked if she might sleep over one day the following week. Her daughter, Mary Beth, had been bored, and like Elizavita, played the piano. It seemed a safe idea. In fact, the visit went very well. There were the odd discussions about bedtime, tidying things up and not rushing her food, but she complied if I teased her.

"The sleep-over went well. No one caught them smoking, but the smell of Elizavita's clothing when she returned betrayed the fact. The Wyman's smoked so they were nose-dead. I didn't, and to me it was obvious.

"Elizavita was affectionate. She'd hold my hand and bump into me when we walked; she'd lean against me watching television; she'd do odd little things like straighten my tie, brush down my jacket with her hands, or tug my cuffs and straighten my cufflinks. Today, alarm bells would be ringing loudly, but they didn't then, and there was nothing improper in anything we said or did."

Damian was emphatic about this. Nothing of the sort had crossed my mind, and I wondered if he protested too much.

"As a treat, towards the end of her last week, I took her into the store. She visited Mrs. Wyman and a few other people she had met, and I let her choose a party dress. Something to take home as a sort of souvenir. She managed to buy a pair of shoes with a heel just a bit higher than fashionable twelve-year-olds were wearing that year."

This struck him as an amusing recollection, and I was happy to see him less agitated than he had been.

"The night before taking her to the airport, I took her to dinner at Butler and Frobisher. I thought it would be a treat to end the week. She surprised me by wearing her new dress, shoes and *makeup*. I hadn't bought her *that*! She was very careful, she had just enough on to be noticeable but not enough to strenuously object to. And that was her art: she could push people hard enough to make them uncomfortable, but not so much as to make their resistance worthwhile."

I considered this. He had obviously formulated this thought over many years until it expressed exactly what he wanted.

"I saw you there," I said, "but I never associated the girl with Ted and Alanna."

Damian nodded.

"She didn't look much like either of them, but she had her mother's coloring. She was at the age when you suspected she could be pretty, but it was no certainty," he mused.

"We enjoyed a good meal and had a pleasant conversation when we got home. The next morning, I drove her to Boston and put her on the flight home. Ted called me later in the day to say she'd arrived safely and had had a wonderful time.

"It was only when tidying her room before Mrs. Hawks came to do the laundry, that I noticed several of my mother's old things that I had moved there missing. There had been a few of her ornaments and things from her dresser: a silver box for rings, a silver-backed mirror, a small Lalique sparrow. I don't suppose they were worth much, but they were gone."

I shook my head.

"Hardly a way to repay kindness," I said.

"I was more saddened than angry," he said, "but it did make me wonder about the life she had. Were things as rosy as had been painted?"

"Ted would have been furious," I said. "I can't think Alanna would have been happy either. What did they say?"

Damian smiled.

"I never told them. Elizavita was gone. Either those things would be a souvenir of her time here, or they would be a reminder of her deception. I could live with either of those cases."

"I think I would have called Ted right away."

"It did occur to me," Damian admitted. "But in a way, it served me right: an old bachelor playing house with a twelve-year-old."

He gave an ironic snort, and went silent.

"But that wasn't the end of it?" I prompted.

It took a moment for him to look up. He looked tired and old.

"No.

"I heard from Ted and Alanna at Christmas. They made a passing reference to some difficulties during the year, but said that Elizavita had continued to talk about her visit. He mentioned some work that would take him away and suggested that Elizavita visit during her February school vacation. She liked snow and hadn't seen much of it.

"I took care to put away the valuables and ornaments that I wanted to keep, and replaced some with a selection of things that had been hidden in drawers and cupboards for years because they had never found favor. Things that had been given to my mother. Ceramic cats, cute owls and souvenirs brought to her by traveling friends. Elizavita could fill her suitcase with them."

I silently applauded his scheme for disposing of unwanted gifts.

"She had grown up, but not as much as I expected. She was still on that edge of being a little girl, albeit a knowing one. What did Nabokov say in *Lolita*? Not human creatures, but demoniac? That was *his* word."

I'd seldom heard Damian make a literary allusion

beyond the clichéd. I suspected he may have read this after Elizavita's previous visit. Forewarned and fore-armed.

"I met her at the airport in Boston and she greeted me like a genuine relative. She chattered all the way back to Westbury telling me about school, her friends, her love of horses and riding, and popular music. We went up to her room, which I had rearranged, in part to camouflage the presence of the new ornaments and the absence of those removed. For a moment, I thought she was going to object, but she sat on the bed and saw that she could look out into the back yard.

"'I can watch the snow when it falls,' she said.

"She seemed happy and I left her to wash and change after her journey. She had a cold drink and cookies while I had a cup of coffee. I had a notepad and asked her what she'd like to do while she was here. I planned to take her into Boston and see the usual sights, and maybe let her ice-skate on one of the ponds. There was already some snow on the ground, but it was only about two inches deep and had been there long enough to lose its freshness.

"She asked if she could call Mary Beth. Fortunately, she did not ask me if Mary Beth could sleep over at my house. The first few days went well. We traveled locally and she and Mary Beth went to a movie, tried bowling and played the piano with each other. They danced to pop music in each other's rooms and talked non-stop.

"She slept at Mary Beth's house, but in the afternoon I had a call from Mrs. Wyman who was furious. She had come home to find Mary Beth and Elizavita smoking in the kitchen and working their way through a bottle of Grand Marnier."

I couldn't resist a chuckle.

"Unfortunately, that was my reaction, too, and Mary Beth was forbidden to come here. Elizavita was similarly banned. I knew they'd still arrange to telephone and meet and regarded it as part of growing up. I collected Elizavita in the car. It was only two blocks away, but she wasn't in the best condition to walk, and she sang all the way home and all the way up to her room.

"When she didn't come down for dinner, I looked in on her. She was fast asleep on her bed, still dressed. I covered her and left her to it. She had a hangover when she surfaced around nine-thirty and was pretty subdued. I rearranged our schedule. Later, she showered and did not reapply the surfeit of makeup she and Mary Beth had decorated themselves with for their cocktail party."

"You must have been counting the days until she went home," I said.

"It's ironic that I saw it as funny at the time while Mrs. Wyman was angry with both girls and with me for thinking it amusing, but years later, when she found it funny, I was unable to laugh."

His voice had grown serious again, and remained so through the rest of his narrative.

"We had our day in Boston. She loved it all: walking the Freedom Trail, eating at Durgin Park, and exploring the Isabella Stewart Gardner Museum. She said it made her feel like a princess. I made Welsh rabbit for supper – she was pleased to see my addition of a splash of sherry – and we talked about the day. I asked how she'd like to spend the following day. I did not offer to take her to Dexter's again, but I did ask if she'd like to go to Butler and Frobisher for dinner. Her eyes lit up at the prospect.

"The next day was cold and dark. Elizavita said she had some reading to do for school and that this was a good morning – and her last chance – to do it. I lit a fire in my study and she curled up in an armchair while I did some work. In the afternoon, she asked if she could go for a walk. I gave her a time to be back, and she wrapped up and went out. I knew she was looking forward to dinner, so I didn't expect any trouble.

"She was back before her scheduled time and set about getting ready for dinner. This was the second time you saw us. When she came down, she looked elegant – and sixteen. Again, she had pushed things about as far as she could with makeup, nylons and heels. Well, I hadn't bought them for her, and she hadn't bought them while she was with me.

"As you and Patricia will have seen, she was

charming company. She ordered sensibly, ate well, and enjoyed the civilized surroundings. She said that it was nice to be away from home for a while; that she thought her world there was boring. I pointed out that Mary Beth, no doubt, found Westbury boring, and she laughed, saying that she did.

"We left the restaurant to find that it had been snowing. Elizavita was delighted to see it and skidded along the sidewalk on the way to the car, trying to catch snowflakes in her mouth. It was a fine snow and was coming down fast. There was no wind, but it was bitterly cold. I started the car and turned up the heat. Elizavita sat quietly inside as I brushed the snow off the car. I drove home very slowly and by the time I put the car in the garage, there was about three inches on the ground.

"'Stay in the garage and I'll bring you some overshoes,' I said to Elizavita.

"'No, don't leave me here,' she said.

"This surprised me as she had never shown the slightest fear of anything. I told her the snow was too deep and would get into her shoes, if she were even able to walk in her heels.

"'Carry me,' she said.

"I could do that. It wasn't far and there were only a few steps. I had decent rubber-soled shoes. She had also said it in her 'don't argue with me' manner. It had been a nice evening and I didn't want to spoil it with an argument. On the other hand, I didn't want her to get away with any pseudo-romantic nonsense. She prepared to climb into my arms, but I threw her over my shoulder in a fireman's lift. She was so shocked that she didn't say a thing until I'd put her down inside and returned to close the garage door."

"How to handle a woman," I said.

"How to handle a manipulative teenager," he retorted. "It was not without consequences. We went into the study where I revived the fire and made her a hot chocolate. I wanted a whisky, but didn't think drinking in front of her was a good idea. She still hadn't given me a reaction to the way I'd carried her, but the hot chocolate soothed her, and she seemed to relax by the fire and was turning the pages of a magazine. We had one more day together and I didn't want her to leave hating me."

Damian's voice slowed and I could sense his reluctance to continue, but I didn't need to prompt him.

"At her usual bedtime, she checked her watch and said she'd be going upstairs.

"'Thank you for a lovely dinner and evening. I like that restaurant, and it was cozy in here,' she said. 'I can watch the snow from my bed.' She kissed my cheek, as she sometimes did, and went to her room.

"By morning, there was about eight inches of snow,

but the wind had picked up and another twelve was predicted. We had breakfast together and listened to the weather report.

"'Will we be able to get to the airport tomorrow?' she asked. I assured her that if the storm stopped in the early evening as predicted, there should be no problems either in getting to Boston or in flying out. I told her about the heated runways, which she thought was amazing.

"I suggested that she get her things together in the morning and if the weather let up, she might like to go out in the afternoon. She was in her room for about an hour before coming down to sit by the fire. I thought she might want to watch television or read, but she just sat, mesmerized by the flames. She seemed content, and I got on with things and then prepared an exciting lunch of tomato soup and grilled cheese sandwiches. To my surprise, she enthused over it and said it was just perfect for a snowy day.

"The snow continued, and the wind was whipping around the house and blowing down the street. The rumble of the snow plows could be heard each hour and they threw up billowing clouds of fine, dry snow before disappearing in their own fog.

"After lunch, Elizavita went upstairs and came down having changed into some warmer clothes.

"'I'm going out,' she announced. 'I want to see Mary

Beth before I go.'

"'I don't think Mrs. Wyman would welcome you,' I said cautiously.

"'Well, I'm going to see her,' she retorted sharply, 'and her mother can't stop me.'

"'You're not going anywhere with that attitude,' I said. I felt it was one of those moments when I'd have to push back.

"'And how are you going to stop me?' she challenged, taking her long blue coat from the rack in the hall.

"'It's bitterly cold, Elizavita,' I said, trying to sound reasonable. 'Wear your warm jacket if you insist on going out.'

"'Why do you try to tell me how to do everything?' she flashed. 'I thought you were different, but you're just like the rest of them!'

"Her explosion came out of the blue. Her face was red with rage, her voice was lower and her bearing was that of a much older girl.

"I didn't know what hit me."

"I should think not," I replied, waiting for him to continue.

"She turned and rushed out the door, slamming it so the house shook, and stomped off down the street."

"Did she go to the Wymans'?"

"I don't know. I reached for the whisky I had forgone

the night before and tried to think how things had so quickly gone off the rails," he said sadly.

"Did you ever work it out?"

"I concluded that things had never really been on the normal track. That somehow it had been wrong from the beginning.

"I never called the Wymans. I figured they could look out for themselves and either let her in, or send her home. However, after six o'clock, I was thinking about supper, and she still hadn't returned. I wondered about calling the police, but even then, I was at a loss as to how to explain the girl's presence – besides, I'd had a few whiskies by then. Enough my colleagues and good friends had thought it curious the year before, and, if I am right, even you and Patricia raised an eyebrow."

He fell silent again.

"The snow and wind had continued. I was worried about her, for no matter why she was there, she was in my trust. I put on my overcoat, scarf, overshoes and gloves and began walking around the neighborhood. I walked past the Wymans' house but there were no lights on. I later learned that they were at Bernard's mother's in Vermont.

"After two hours of walking around the neighborhood, I was frozen and frightened. The snow was still swirling and the wind was bitter. This girl needed to catch a flight in Boston before noon the next day. I couldn't tell Ted that I'd lost her. I plodded home praying that I'd find her on the doorstep. I wouldn't even mind if she were angry.

"I stayed up until midnight hoping to hear a knock on the door or receive a phone call. Eventually, there was nothing to do but go to bed and hope I'd wake up and find it was all a nightmare."

Damian was now relating the story with obvious difficulty. He knew how thin his excuses for doing nothing sounded and that the next words out of my mouth would be ones of harsh condemnation.

However, I didn't want to interrupt him or distract him from the rest of his story.

"I awoke to a beautiful, sunny morning. The world outside was so glorious that the events of the previous evening could not have been real. I dressed and knocked on Elizavita's door and called to her.

"Of course, there was no response. She had not come back, although I had left the doors unlocked. I looked around the room. Her suitcase was on the bed, partially packed and her black dress lay next to it as a reminder of her presence. I looked around again to see if there might be any clue as to where she had gone, and I was shocked to see that all the objects she had taken the year before had been returned to their former places.

"Filled with confusion and dread, I knew there was nothing to do except resume my search for her and try to think of what to say to Ted and Alanna. I would certainly have to go to the police now.

"I walked the streets around my house in increasing circles, as I had done the night before. The snow before the Wymans' was still unbroken. There was no sign of there ever having been footprints, so it was doubtful that Elizavita had ever tried to see Mary Beth.

It was now past the time when we should have left for the airport. Feeling sick, I resolved to call the police when I got home. Although I had come out my front door, I now walked around the house to the back door so as not to track snow through the front hall. As I looked into the back yard – "

Here, his voice gave out. I said nothing but waited for him to recover himself.

"As I looked into the back yard, the sun caught a small mound covered in snow. Its rounded top suggested that it wasn't a normal snow drift, but that the snow had fallen on something lying on the ground.

"I went inside, closed the curtains and sat staring at the cold fireplace. I thought of only two things: what I would do when the telephone rang with Ted calling to see why his daughter wasn't on the flight, and how I would kill myself."

His hand was shaking now as he reached to his forehead. He looked at me like someone who had been lost for a very long time, and I was powerless to help him.

"Hours went by, but the telephone never rang.

"I dragged myself to bed and once again prayed that I would awake from a dream. The next morning was just as clear and bright. I opened the curtains with trepidation, leaving the one at the back of the house until last.

"The snowy shape was still there. Pristine and glistening. I felt mocked by its brilliance and sickened by what lay beneath. I would have to do something. Even in its frozen state, a body would attract animals.

"Several times, I put on my boots and coat to do what I knew I had to, but each time, I failed and cursed my cowardice. Was this what I had come to? Someone who was intimidated by a thirteen-year-old and shadows?

"Curiously, the telephone didn't ring that day. I tried making a few calls, and the line was working, so I couldn't understand why I had not heard from Ted.

"A week went by. More snow fell, and the shape grew larger and with it my feeling of dread. None of this was making any sense, but there was no doubt in my mind that it was only a matter of time before the police arrived, or Ted himself. Yet, none of that happened.

"The time came when I dragged myself back to work and went through the motions of my job. Everyone could see that I had changed in some way, even when I thought I was putting on a pretty good show of being normal.

"Inevitably, I ran into the Wymans. Mrs. Wyman had calmed down and even joked about the Grand Marnier incident.

"'At least it was a drink with some class,' she said. 'Has Elizavita gone home now?'

"'She's gone,' was all I could manage.

"A week. Two weeks passed and I had heard nothing from Ted and Alanna. It was mid-March, and although we had had more snow, it was beginning to melt. Each day the snow thinned, I knew my time as a free man was also melting away.

"In an audacious move, I wrote a note to Ted and Alanna saying how much I enjoyed her company and hoped she had enjoyed herself as much this year as last. It was probably too little, too late, but I felt I had to make some sort of effort at contacting them.

"One evening, the weather forecast was for warm air to come up from the south and deliver a lot of rain. This would be it. It would melt and wash away the snow and that would be that. The rain started at about eight and I listened to it as I lay in bed and imagined what it was washing away. It was still raining in the morning and I had to get up and go to work. I opened my bedroom curtains, and all but a few isolated piles of compacted snow from neighbors' driveways and front walks had gone and brown lawns appeared up and down the street.

"It took all my strength to get up, dress for work and nibble a piece of toast. I had not eaten well since she had gone. Indeed, I had not done many of my usual things and was beginning to be missed. People would call about missing this meeting or that club. Each time the phone rang, my stomach turned.

"When it was time to leave, it was with a combination of fascination and terror that I opened the back door and looked to the back lawn.

"All the snow had gone and there was nothing there."

My mouth opened, but I didn't say anything.

"You would have thought that I would be over-whelmed with relief. No. I was overwhelmed with fear.

"I went through the day like a – what are they called in films?"

"Zombies."

"That's it. Moving without will or comprehension. Several colleagues wanted me to see a doctor immed-iately. I resisted that, but did leave an hour early so as to get home in daylight and take a good look around. I don't know what I expected to find. Drag marks; animal footprints? I don't know, but I knew I needed to inspect my property thoroughly.

"I did that, picking up bits of broken branches that had come down over the winter, but essentially, everything was as it should be. I began to doubt all of it.

I went in, put on the kettle and went upstairs to change out of my business suit. I couldn't resist a glance into Elizavita's room, but it was as it had been.

"Downstairs, I made tea and carried it into my study before returning to the hallway to pick up the small pile of mail that was on the floor.

"I gathered them up and saw a familiar envelope. It was the letter I had sent to Ted.

"On the envelope was written, 'Moved. Left no forwarding address. Return to sender.'"

The Night Before Christmas

Thoughts and Whispers

The Night Before Christmas

Christmas 1971

The Isle of Capri remains, after thousands of years, a fickle muse. Stepping on to its shore, one can never be certain of the island's reaction. She treated Odysseus badly, and Tiberius well. It is a secretive island; a chaste rock which, no matter how well one thinks one knows it, is always hiding some virtue – or vice.

It is an Italian island, not a predictable Greek one which indicates love or hate within an hour of landing. It is an island of passion and secrets. Its temper may be docile or explosive; its decision to embrace or reject is seemingly random, for it does not necessarily reward the virtuous or punish the wicked. Perhaps it is not a question of good or evil, but rather the feeling or aura of the visitor. Whatever the case, the visitor to Capri will never feel indifference towards it.

Why did Ambrose Nutpool choose to come to Capri? He came to escape. He was a failure.

Nutpool wasn't the sort to get himself into trouble deliberately, no one with the name of Nutpool would. Circumstances would play against him almost deliberately, and his lack of extra-ordinary ability further hindered his progress. Had Nutpool known Maugham's story, he may have recognised Thomas Wilson and identified with his fate.

Somehow he had managed to survive the education more or less beaten into him at one of London's more brutal East End secondary moderns and he had enlisted in the Army. After two years of blind obedience and unquestioning service to his superiors, he found himself named in a court martial involving the disappearance of several thousand pounds worth of equipment. The questioning, the responsibility and the guilt were passed down the chain of command, and in due process, Nutpool was summarily discharged.

With a record of dishonour, larceny and embezzlement, it was impossible for Nutpool to find employment anywhere. There was only one final option. He went to Cambridge to read Economics.

Nutpool wasn't stupid, slow-witted or foolish; he was merely so detached from reality that no one who had known him could ever imagine him having a family – mother, father, wife or children. He was the sort who one wanted to see twenty years hence, just to see how he made out.

Nutpool's reputation spread quickly through the Cambridge court yards and he was promptly made treasurer of several organisations. Inevitably, in the middle of his second year, no trace of any of the monies entrusted to his care could be found, and he was sent down.

He resolved to go on a grand tour. He couldn't afford it, but he had nothing else to do, so one afternoon, he got on a train in Victoria and began his journey. He had very few clothes and spent two full weeks on trains. He began to forget what it was like to sleep in a horizontal position.

He was rattling across France when he resolved to spend Christmas in Capri. The basis for this decision was the mere sound of the words: Christmas in Capri. He had heard someone in Cambridge utter them one night at a dinner and thought they had a marvellous ring. It also had a fashionable sound to it, far more acceptable than "cashiered from the Army," or "sent down from Cambridge", though the latter was not without redeeming merit. Thus, at six in the evening of the twenty-fourth of December, Ambrose Nutpool arrived on Capri, not knowing what to expect, and, in general, not caring. He was grateful to be off the Italian National Railway.

Had he not been starving upon his arrival, the course of his life might have been substantially different. As it was, he had existed for the past several days on warm beer and *panettone* sold on the trains at Christmas time. He had accumulated a collection of the square blue boxes and had amused himself by piling them in different arrangements in his compartment. So, as soon as he found a cheap room with a horizontal bed, he began to look for some place to eat.

He crossed the town square and looked in the windows of several restaurants which were closed because it was Christmas eve. He found a narrow walk from the square which wound along until he thought he was beyond civilisation. He was about to return to the square to try another street when he saw a yellow light glowing ahead. He walked on and found that it came from an illuminated sign which displayed the menu of a restaurant which, presumably, was in the nearby building.

Though not fond of seafood, Nutpool decided that he'd find nothing better. He descended a few steps, followed a paved walk which passed beneath an arch of fragrant vines and went down a final short flight of steps into the restaurant. He stood in the doorway for a moment. There were a few couples at scattered tables. It looked good enough, perhaps too good, as it was the cleanest restaurant he had seen since leaving London.

A man approached him. It could have been Hercule Poirot, for he sported a goatee and a neatly trimmed black moustache. He said nothing, but gave a sweep of his hand indicating that he could choose his table. When he was seated, the man gave him a menu which he read carefully. It was all in English except for the prices and the name of the restaurant: Taverna Satana. "No wonder it's open Christmas eve," Nutpool thought. "That also accounts for the general brilliance of the place."

The walls were finished with glazed tiles with flame patterns. The woods were dark and the table cloths a light orange. There was certainly nothing sinister about the atmosphere, nor of any of the people. The couple in the corner Nutpool recognised as the Americans he had seen on the ferry from Naples. There was a German couple across from him, and two women (retired teachers) farther away.

"Are you ready to order?" the man asked with a French accent. He gave his order and relaxed to a four course dinner. It was nearly ten-thirty o'clock when he finished his meal. He walked over to the bar where the Frenchman was polishing glasses. "Was your meal satisfactory?"

"Very good, thank you. May I have the bill?"

"Certainly, monsieur," he turned to get his order book.

"Wait – just a moment; I think I'd like some coffee and maybe a brandy."

"Certainly, monsieur. Would you like it at your table?"

"No. Here is fine, if you don't mind."

"Pull up a stool."

He gave him the brandy and coffee. "Are you on Capri for long?"

"I don't know."

"You have friends here?"

"I have friends nowhere."

The Frenchman poured himself a drink.

"Santé."

"Cheers."

"You sound down and out for such a young man," the Frenchman ventured. "Are you out of work? Have you lost a girl?"

"Why do you ask?"

"Just making conversation. It is a quiet night. Christmas eve is always a quiet night. So is Good Friday. We don't have to talk if you don't want to."

"It's all right. I don't mind. I'm just suspicious of people who ask a lot of questions."

"You've been in trouble with those types before?"

"Yes," Nutpool sighed. "Look, if I'm going to tell you my life story over this brandy, I'd better introduce myself. My name is Nutpool. Ambrose Nutpool."

"And I am Jacques Clufier."

"Good to meet you. How did you happen to come to Capri?"

"No, no, my friend. Your story first."

Nutpool talked to Clufier for about an hour, explaining his various misfortunes and unparalleled bad luck. They drained several glasses of brandy and finished the pot of coffee.

When Nutpool finished his narration, he stood up to leave.

"You'll want to close. I've been rambling on about my problems for an hour and you've been very patient. I shan't be a bore."

"No, don't leave – that is, unless you want to. I am not bored. Besides, you have yet to hear my story.

"You intrigue me, for you have met with great misfortune and injustice. By right, you should be a success. But, we'll talk of that later. Here is how I came to Capri: . . . ."

Monsieur Clufier gave a broadly painted picture of his upbringing in the south of France; his education at the Sorbonne and his service in the war.

"I was working with the underground in 1943 when I came in contact with an unusual group of agents near Chartres. It was a group of agents I have remained associated with ever since. In fact, my dear Nutpool, I think this group might be able to help you. If you're willing."

"If it's some sort of religious organisation, I can't say that I'd be very interested. Thank you just the same."

"No, it's not a religious organisation," M. Clufier said with a chuckle. "I'd be suspicious, too, if it were."

"Go on, then."

"My dear Nutpool, there are ways of getting nearly everything in this world. The ways *not* at our disposal would only get us things we wouldn't want anyway."

Clufier moistened his finger in the brandy and rubbed it round the rim of the snifter.

Nutpool watched the finger go round and round and heard the ringing of the glass increase intensity. It echoed off the tile walls until the room was filled with sound. As he stared at the glass, the brandy seemed to glow. First it was just a luminescent reddish brown, but then the brown seemed to fade, leaving a full deep red colour. M. Clufier slowed the movement of his hand and the original colour of the brandy was restored. He had seen it all with perfect clarity.

"Clufier! Is it really possible?" Nutpool asked in a hoarse whisper.

"All things are possible," he replied. "All you must do is take advantage of every situation; you cannot help but be successful."

"Ha! What do you, or your unusual group, want in return? There isn't much I can call my own that is of any value."

Clufier laughed.

"I don't want anything," Clufier said.

"Nothing?"

"Nothing at all."

"I don't promise anything?" Nutpool asked incredulously. "Really?"

"No. Nothing. Just go back to England and make your fortune."

"I didn't promise anything. I didn't promise anything."

Nutpool repeated these words to himself many times, both on his way back to his hotel and after his return to England.

He had been in England for about a week without having had any great inspirations of how to make a fortune. He was almost out of money and about to dismiss the whole incident in Capri as nonsense. He went to a pub one evening and resolved to temporally obliterate his difficulties.

It was an ordinary pub. Nutpool had been there many times before and recognised many of the faces along the bar and at the tables. He stood by himself and watched the people round him and listened to bits of conversation.

"Of course he knew about her. Why else would he have married her – ?"

"I never won a farthing on anything and this twit comes along and makes five hundred quid in the pools. I ask you, what's he need with more money – ?"

"What galls me is that he isn't qualified to do anything. It's us, people like you and me, who have worked for years – and we end up working for him who

Thoughts and Whispers

can't do a thing but live off our sweat – "

Nutpool focused on this conversation. It was between two men who looked like construction workers of some sort. One was heavy set with thin hair and the other, the speaker, was tall and thin and had dark bushy eyebrows.

"Can he put two bricks together and make 'em stand up? My arse! He sits in his glass tower and collects money and puts his name on our work. It ain't fair and it ain't right."

Nutpool had another drink. He considered what the men had said. The situation applied to him, too. He couldn't do anything either. He pondered this a while before deciding that he was executive material.

In his room that night, he constructed a plan. All it took was nerve, and since he had nothing to begin with, he had nothing to lose.

In the early hours of the morning, he took step one and burgled a shop in Jermyn Street taking several pin-stripe suits, a coat, two hats, three shirts, two pairs of shoes and an umbrella.

At nine o'clock he paid for a shave, hair-cut and manicure at the Ritz Hotel, picked a rose from Green Park and walked to the best known estate agents in the Strand.

Before noon, he had examined and signed the lease for eight thousand square feet of office space, leaving the manager a list of specifications for carpeting, lighting and furnishing.

"A sign, Mr Nutpool?"

"Sign? Yes, of course. On the doors, five inches high, 'A. Nutpool and Associates, Solicitors.'"

"Very good, sir."

"Can all this be ready by March 15? We have to vacate our current premises."

"It'll be ready, sir."

From the office building, Nutpool went to a phone box and called the major newspapers and ordered ads announcing the move to new offices, and the availability of positions for recently qualified solicitors and legal secretaries.

He interviewed everyone at the American Bar of the Savoy.

When the ides of March rolled round, Nutpool had engaged no fewer than a dozen young solicitors and half a dozen secretaries.

On bright new stationery, but in the best possible taste, Nutpool wrote several London Clubs and proposed membership for his solicitors.

Every one was accepted.

The opening of the new offices was reported in the papers. Two even published his photograph.

The first weeks were squeakers. A bank loan was negotiated through a carefully cultivated acquaintance at a club, and that saw Nutpool and Associates through the first few months. Then, money began coming in. Sometimes Nutpool was near desperation, but the money came in at the last minute.

By the end of the first year, Nutpool and Associates showed a healthy bank balance, and all loans were repaid.

Ambrose Nutpool continued to conduct business in a similar manner for several years. The company's yearly profit was regular, but Nutpool felt it was rather stagnant. He was dissatisfied and called one of his closest associates into his office.

"Harrison, our profits are not showing enough growth."

"Well sir, we reached our optimum level in our second year. We've held on since then."

"Suppose we hired more lawyers?"

"Our overheads would go up proportionally."

"What, then, Harrison, is the solution?"

"To make other investments."

"But I only want to invest in Nutpool and Associates," Nutpool said fiercely. "Can't we attract new business? Large corporations?"

"We're not big enough for that. Anyway, most large organisations have in-house legal departments."

"Let me work on it," Nutpool said and dismissed him.

It wasn't the sort of thinking to be done in the office. Nutpool walked along the streets and found himself by the pub where he had received his inspiration five years before. He ordered a pint and sat in the corner.

The crowd looked much the same. There was a team of workers in for lunch. Nutpool spoke to the one next to him.

"Where are you working?"

"Up at the Inner City College. Some geezer's given them a library."

"That's a nice gift."

"No, it ain't. It's some politician wot's been stealing us blind for years. 'Is conscience is got the best of him, sos 'e's doing somefink for his old manor. But it's you and me wot's paid for it and it makes 'im look like a statesman." Nutpool bought him a drink. It had worked again. The germ of an idea came to him. Back at the office, he called Harrison.

"I've got it, Harrison. We're going to make a bundle. I'm going to give a library to Redcliffe Hall."

"Is that your school?"

"Good God, no. But they're one of the richest ones and they could use a new wing to their library. It shouldn't cost more than a few hundred thousand."

"But we haven't got – "

"Details, details. Listen, Harrison. I make a big

announcement that I'm giving a library to Redcliffe. We'll get their legal business. I'll get the business of the architectural firm I choose and of the construction company. The publicity will bring in new business and the building won't cost us a thing."

"But the overheads – "

"We cultivate a portfolio of rich customers who require expensive work. Our small stuff can be given to a handful of the junior boys."

"You're mad. It'll never work."

But it did.

There was a time when the construction company was demanding money in payment, but Nutpool halted the work "to make revisions in the design." By stalling the progress, he could also stall payment.

Profits for the year during which Ambrose Nutpool gave away a library had never been higher.

The publicity had other spin-offs: Nutpool was asked to become a director of several companies and a trustee of various institutions. Obviously, he became a governor of Redcliffe Hall. He also married Vanessa, daughter of the merchant banker, Forbes Gordon-Forbes-Gordon.

There was certainly no need now to continue his risk-taking and over-extending, but he had come to like the challenge of it. It offered him something to think about. His organisation was a beautiful bubble, pumped up by the egos of everyone involved.

He began to enjoy his wealth. For the first time, he began to spend money on himself. He bought houses, automobiles, expensive clothes and jewellery for his wife. He kept a mistress in Hampstead.

One day, Georgia, his mistress, told him he was working too hard and should take a vacation, adding that she had never been to Majorca.

"If I take you to Majorca, I shall have to take my wife around the world."

"Tell her you're going on business. Give some school in Majorca a new building."

"But who will be in charge here?"

"*I want to go to Majorca!*"

Nutpool took Georgia to Majorca, then took his wife to Wales. He was away from his offices for six weeks, during which Harrison took over. When Nutpool returned, he announced that he was giving buildings to both a school in Wales and a medical clinic in Palma.

However, things were not going well at the office. Harrison had made a thorough study of the books in Nutpool's office.

"This whole company is a fraud!" Harrison shrieked.

"Oh, Harrison. Don't pretend you just worked that out. You were in the office the day I decided to give my first library."

"That was a business gamble. You don't need to

make the sort of gambles you do. When I saw that you began the organisation with – nothing! Absolutely nothing. You're not even a solicitor yourself."

"Never said I was," Nutpool replied, then paused. "How much are you making, Harrison?"

Harrison told him.

"Could you have done as well anywhere else at your age?"

"No."

"Have you ever doubted where your money came from?"

"No."

"Then get out of my office and get back to work."

"Oh, I'll get out of your office. I'll get out of your entire stinking organisation."

"I wouldn't be too hasty."

"I'm going to put you out of business."

"Poor Harrison. You really don't understand these things."

Harrison left Nutpool and Associates. From time to time people asked what became of him, because he was never seen again. Anywhere.

Nutpool was made a CBE in the January honours. Later that spring, he took Georgia to Barcelona and his wife to Inverness.

Construction costs had now risen so high that Nutpool was forced to cut down his building programme. His final major project was going to cost nearly five million pounds, but its phased construction was spread over a five year period during which he could easily raise the necessary brass – assuming that things continued as they had in the past.

Things did not continue as they had. Increased taxation, runaway inflation and the sky- rocketing oil prices all came on top of the property collapse. Then, there were the restricting currency exchange controls.

"Ambrose, you're so on edge," said Georgia one night.

"I'm running out of money."

"Never!" she laughed.

"It's true. By the end of next week, I must make a payment for the Centre of ten thousand pounds and I have not got it."

"You've been in spots like this before."

"Yes, I know; but I have never had so much to lose before."

He stopped and laughed.

"When I began, it was a great risk, but I had nothing to lose; in reality it was perfectly safe. Now I have everything: wealth (supposedly), position, family and all, and I cannot afford to lose."

"You must have faith, my darling. You've always made it before."

"I'm going to have to grab what I can and make a

run for it."

"I'm coming with you. Shall we move to Spain?"

"Anywhere."

In the next week, Nutpool was discreet in making flight reservations to Barcelona and converted his remaining money into drafts payable at a Spanish bank. He filled his briefcase with ten-pound notes.

"Faith," he mumbled to himself. "Who ever heard of having faith in the devil? Can't trust anyone these days."

It was two days before the payment was due and the day before Nutpool's flight to Barcelona. He walked down to his pub. He hadn't been there for years, but it was still the same. He ordered a pint.

"Ambrose!" a man called to him.

"Sir James," Nutpool answered.

"I'll bet you're here to celebrate. It's almost a certainty, isn't it?"

"What's that?"

"You don't have to play dumb with me, old boy. You really don't know, do you?"

"No, Sir James, I really don't."

"Well, that's what you get for running out of Parliament when the session adjourns. There is a very good chance – a certainty, really – of your firm being named solicitors for this government."

"Solicitors for the government?"

"Times are changing."

"Solicitors for the government?"

"A prevalent rumour, dear boy. Should be announced any day now."

Nutpool returned to the office. He scanned the papers and called in the senior members of the firm. No one had heard the story. He called some fellow MPs. None of them admitted to hearing it either.

He visited Georgia that evening.

"I told you to have faith, darling."

"But I can't afford to take that risk. Unless it's in the morning papers, we're going to be on that plane."

"Can't you change the reservation for Friday?"

"I can't be in the country on Friday and not be at the office. Someone will know something is wrong."

"Can you mail the cheque and hope for the announcement before the banks open Monday?"

"No. I've always dealt with these people in person. If I'm not there, everyone will know something's wrong."

"I still say, you've got to have more faith in yourself."

"Poor Georgia. You really don't understand a thing."

"I'll be with you."

"Ten o'clock. Heathrow terminal two."

Like all of Nutpool's plans, his escape came off perfectly.

No one questioned either of them, and it is doubtful that he was missed by the office until the evening papers came out. They announced that the government had chosen Nutpool and Associates as Solicitors for the Government.

When the air mail *Times* reached Nutpool's room in his Barcelona hotel, the front page carried the twin stories:

Government's Legal Firm Collapses in Fraud: Executive Flees Country with West End Model

On the heels of the Nutpool collapse, came the collapse of the government itself.

"Another inevitable page of British history," Nutpool said sardonically. "It all sounds painfully familiar."

"We'll be all right, darling."

"How's your Spanish?"

Nutpool was fifty years old when he fled to Spain. He had given fourteen libraries, six hospital wings and part of an apartment and shopping complex. These buildings had been paid for by the architects who designed them; the contractors who built them; the institutions who received them; and, satisfyingly, the banks that financed them. They had cost Nutpool nothing and brought him hundreds of thousands. It had been his lack of faith which brought his downfall. He knew this and it haunted him until the end of his life.

Spain made him sick. Everything about it.

After six years of bull-fights, flamenco, sangria and paella, Nutpool had a severe stroke.

Georgia had stayed with him and remained at his bedside during his moments of consciousness. He was incoherent most of the time, but could be heard repeating the same phrase over and over again, "I never promised anything; I never promised. . . ."

Thoughts and Whispers

Indian Summer
A Westbury Tale

Thoughts and Whispers

Indian Summer
A Westbury Tale

L ooking for things to do now that I have retired, I guess it's time to record a bit of family history. Every family has subjects it doesn't talk about. They may be such skeletons as a family member who drank, who had an affair, who embezzled, who did drugs, or was caught feeding the birds, stark naked in a public park at four in the morning and was never seen again.

This story is different, and I want to set it down while I can. There's no family left to object, and while there is no reason for it to have been embarrassing, and no one was hurt, it was something that was never spoken of.

In the summer of 1962, my father changed jobs and began teaching history at Westbury College, in north central Massachusetts, towards the New Hampshire border. Westbury, for those who don't know it, is a city smaller than Worcester, perhaps the same size as Springfield, and has an industrial past that is typical of those cities and a dozen more in New England.

My father had grown up in Westbury and, while acknowledging that the city wasn't a beautiful center of social aspirations, he saw its character and loved the fact

239

that you could get between the city and the country quickly. My mother, from Scranton, Pennsylvania, couldn't see the appeal. To her, Westbury was Scranton with worse winters. However, her attitude changed when they found the farm. Our house was always called "the farm," though by the 1960s, it hadn't been a working farm for a hundred years.

The farm as we knew it, was a hundred acres of woods that had stone fences and paths running through it. Our woods joined the woods of a similar farm far enough away that we never saw it, and extended into the limitless forests of northern Massachusetts and southern New Hampshire.

Even today, looking at Google Maps, you can see that you can go ten miles north – straight – from the house and not cross any sort of road. It's not much different going east and west. We were about half a mile from a country road that led into Westbury. In spite of the remote sound of the location, it took Dad about twenty minutes to get to his department, even with morning traffic.

As children, we didn't know much about the history of the house, though Dad explained it to us several times as we were growing up. My two brothers were older than me. I was eight when we moved to the farm. Dale was fourteen and Steve was eleven. That made us an odd lot. Dale and Steve were far enough apart in age for them not to have much in common. However, throw an eight-year-old girl into the mix, and Dale and Steve turned into best friends.

I can't complain. When we moved to the farm, Mom and Dad showed us around. There was lots to explore, and they were happy to let us, but there were rules. One of them was we couldn't go out of sight of the house alone. The other was never to try to "lose" one of us or our friends in the woods. Hide and seek had to be within sight of the house. We were to know at all times where the other people with us were.

I have to say, we followed these rules. Dale and Steve never tried to lose me, or even scare me in the woods. We'd tell stories to each other. We'd take a "picnic lunch" into the woods together – usually a sandwich, some potato chips, a piece of fruit and a drink – and do things that we wouldn't do if our parents were with us, like run on the top of the old walls.

We had a lot of fun, though by the time I was fifteen if a boyfriend and I planned to venture into the woods, my mother would send Dale or Steve along if they were around. Otherwise, we'd have to stay in sight of the house.

The house itself was pretty typical. It was a Cape Cod style, but without second floor dormers. Instead, there was a large extension that held the kitchen and, upstairs, a bathroom and several bedrooms. There was a porch that looked over a lawn and some old fruit trees. Every year, we'd try to eat the apples, but they hadn't been looked after for so long they were virtually wild.

I didn't pay attention to any of the house's history, then. I was more interested in what color my room was going to be painted. I did know that the house was very old. It creaked at night and in the early morning when the heat came on. It was reckoned that it was built in about 1790. It had been remodeled and restored a few times, but I think most of it was real.

For all of us, who had been living in an apartment in Lowell, being surrounded by woods was a big change. While it was neat that there was all that space and places to explore, there were bits about it that were scary.

We'd been used to the noise of traffic, people coming and going, airplanes, freight trains at night, other people's televisions and music. What we weren't used to was the near silence and unexpected animal noises. It didn't seem to bother Dale, but one day when Steve and I were walking to see the stream that ran near one of the paths, he admitted that sometimes he felt uneasy.

The stream was only a few hundred yards from the house, but it was deep enough in the woods that we couldn't see it or hear anything. Steve had taken a few of Mom's pie tins from the cupboard as he'd had this idea that we pan for gold in the stream and we'd all be rich. We had no idea how to do it, and little idea what we were looking for, but we stood in the stream, our toes sinking deeper into the soft bottom, and took turns going through the motions.

It must have been late August because it was hot, and the stream was shallow and moving so slowly that it hardly made a sound. It trickled down the gradual hill over stones that had been too small to use in the fences or for building. While I was bent over spilling water and sand over myself, Steve sat on the bank gazing into the trees.

"We should follow the stream and see where it comes from," I said, thinking it was a good idea.

He nodded.

"Shall we do it?" I asked.

"One day."

I couldn't understand his lack of enthusiasm.

"When?" I persisted.

"We should do it with Dale," he said.

"Why? We could do it now," I said.

That's when he admitted that sometimes – not all the time, he stressed, but sometimes – the woods made him uneasy.

I remember vividly what he said because it was the first time either of my brothers indicated that they weren't really Superman.

"I don't know," he said. "I guess it's because I don't know what's out there."

He had said it in a thoughtful way, but it really frightened me. I don't know why. I'm not easily startled or frightened.

The way the upstairs of the house was built, the rooms were at the end of hallways that wrapped around the large central chimney. There were no fireplaces upstairs, but there were ones in the dining room and living room, and my parents suspected there was an old oven behind a wall that had been boarded over. The upstairs room arrangement meant that none of us were near each other and had to walk some distance to get to the bathroom from our bedrooms. Anyway, I was on my own and wasn't scared, even during thunderstorms.

Well, most thunderstorms.

Moving had meant that we would start at new schools, which Dale and Steve thought was exciting. I was less sure, but that was still weeks away, and the summer was perfect to continue our explorations and help our parents move and rearrange furniture.

The painters moved through the house quickly. Maybe they didn't, I don't suppose I was paying much attention to them at that age. All I remember is that they were out of the house a few weeks before school started. There were lots of bare walls everywhere, but some of them looked nice. There was a creamy yellow in the living room that I remember seemed to change color during the day as the light changed. In the morning, it was quite light, but by evening, it was a rich mustard and gave the room a warm, cozy feeling.

It was a hot summer – they all are in childhood – and we spent a lot of time in the cooler woods exploring, and later flopped on the porch, sucking a popsicle and drifting back and forth on an old sort of couch that swung on a metal frame. Mom called it a glider. I could sit on it for hours, silently gliding back and forth. Sometimes, I'd push it hard back to the stops and then pick up my feet and see how long it took to become perfectly still again. Best was when someone else was on it with me and they did all the pushing, and I could just curl up, but that was mostly during my teenage years.

We continued to discover things bit by bit. There was an old dump about three hundred feet from the house. There wasn't much of interest there apart from old colored bottles that we used to dig for with sticks. We'd make the kitchen sink muddy cleaning them until Mom told us to clean them in the stream or pond. It was a very small pond, a temporary stop for the water before it trickled out again. At one time the odd migrating duck might have found it, but now whatever fields there had been were dense woodland. The boys joked about making a swimming pool there. One of the small towns had converted the basement of an old mill into a municipal swimming pool, fed by the mill pond. Dale had been there with friends and said that when you swam underwater you could see bricked up windows from the old building.

One of the things we did was try to work out what our farm would have looked like when it was a farm. There were no fields any more, and no barn or stables. There was a covered area where wagons or carriages might have parked, but no sign of any stalls for the horses. Mom and Dad parked their cars there.

We didn't know if there had been animals besides the horses, or if the farm was just for growing crops, vegetables and some fruit. There was still quite a lot of fruit around, but not enough to sell. There were apple trees dotted around. Mom cooked with the small and sour apples once in a while, but their small size meant they were more work than they were worth. There was a curious tree at the bottom of the lawn (almost a hundred feet from the house). It was an old apple tree that had two main branches. The divide was low enough that I could climb up and sit in the cleft. Since the two branches were thick, there was little chance of falling off, so sometimes I take a book with me and just disappear for the afternoon. What we discovered in the spring was the two sections of the tree flowered at completely different times, and when the fruit came, they were two different types of apple. The trees must have been twisted together more than a hundred years ago and although they grew together, they kept their identity.

Anyway, looking for clues from the old farm: When the brush was cleared and the grass cut from the areas around the house, we found a raised stone platform. Dad said it was the old well. The top had been covered with large flat stones and cement. Dale wondered how many bodies were down there, but even I didn't take that seriously enough to let it frighten me. Mom eventually put some large pots of flowers on it and after a few years of cutting, grass began to fill in the area and it became just another part of the yard.

We did find some marks on the outside of the garage that Dale and Steve thought showed where a lean-to roof might have been. Dale thought it might have been a stable, but we didn't find anything else. Later when Dale was learning about archaeology at school, we had an expedition and a dig around the "stable" area but didn't find anything. Not surprising, it was only one Saturday afternoon.

Towards the end of that first summer, Mom and Dad, fed up with painting trim inside, saying they could do that all winter, started working outside in the evenings and on weekends. They decided they wanted to open one old field that was behind the house. They'd cut out all the undergrowth and left the oldest trees and any young ones that would eventually fill in the more open areas. What they found was that even though it had, presumably, been an open field or paddock, it was still full of rocks. Dad said it was likely that they had worked themselves out of the ground since the field had stopped being used.

Needless to say, moving the rocks became our job. I couldn't carry much, but Dale and Steve moved a lot, though even after several evenings of working with our parents, it was hard to see much difference, although the fences were about a foot taller.

This clearance work made us explore a little beyond the walls of that field, just on the other side of them. It was just more woods; more undergrowth and more rocks. We were thrashing about being silly one Sunday afternoon when all of a sudden, Steve gave a cry.

"Dale! Molly! Come look at this!"

It was something he often shouted when he found a snakeskin, or a bird's nest, or some other interesting discovery. His voice had an added urgency this time. We look towards him a few hundred feet in front of us, but still near the wall. He was standing looking up at a tree.

Dale and I rushed to him, but tried not to make too much noise, as we thought he'd seen a bird or other animal and didn't want to scare it away.

Having shouted to us once, he just stood there with his mouth open and his eyes fixed.

We stood next to him and looked up.

Stuck into the tree over our heads, about seven feet up, was an arrow.

We stared at it in silence, then Steve jumped and reached for it. He didn't come close, and Dale pulled him down anyway.

"Don't touch it!" he instructed. "You might break it. We'll get Dad."

Why do parents never come when they're called, but children are always supposed to? We ran into the house, all talking at once about Indians in the woods but Dad just told us that it was 4-4 in the bottom of the eighth and the Red Sox actually had a chance of winning. This was enough for the boys, and they sat on the sofa with him. Mom was in a chair sewing buttons on shirts, darning socks or patching knees, so I wasn't able to do much except sit on the floor and watch the endless game.

When the Red Sox finally lost, Dale and Steve had calmed down so much that it seemed they had forgotten what we found. They were arguing about the game and started to go to the kitchen with Mom for a cold drink when I blurted:

"There are Indians in the woods!"

Whether the silence was because of what I said, or that I had yelled it, I wasn't sure, but it brought Dale and Steve back to life.

"Yeah! She's right," Dale said, excitedly. "Come on out!"

I don't know what Mom and Dad thought we'd found, but they gave their, "We'll humor them," look to each other and followed us out of the house.

We led them through the clear wood and clambered over the wall. When it took us a minute to find the right tree, I thought Dad was going to go back into the house.

"There it is!" Steve called.

We all stood, looking at a very old arrow stuck into an even older tree.

After a moment, Dale, Steve and I shifted our gaze to our parents who continued to stare without speaking, their disbelief complete. It was almost another full minute before my father moved to look at the arrow from different angles. It was high enough up the tree that he could walk under it.

"Can you get the camera, Pat," he finally said.

"Do you think it's real?" Mom asked before going.

"Oh, yes," Dad said softly. "Look how the bark has grown around the arrowhead. There's even something left of the fletching."

We tried to look but it was too high for us to see easily.

The three of us now sat on the wall while we waited for Mom to come back with the camera. Dad continued to look around the tree.

"I'm going to get a ladder. Dale, you can help me."

They went off and Steve and I waited on the wall. Steve was very quiet, so I nudged him.

"Mom and Dad looked really scared," he said unsteadily.

"They weren't scared," I said. "They were just surprised that we'd discovered something so cool."

They *were* scared, but I didn't want to admit it. Why were they scared if that had been there for a long time? I didn't *really* think there were Indians in the woods. Anyway, the Indians around here had been friendly, hadn't they? I'd seen the cowboys and Indian movies with the boys and the TV shows, but the bad ones were way out West. The ones around here had helped the Pilgrims. Right?

The others came back quickly with the camera and ladder. They decided Mom would take the pictures because she knew best how to use the camera. Dad held the ladder for her. She took as many shots as she had film for, but also managed to get one of us standing on the wall with the tree and arrow showing in the background.

Dale and Steve took the ladder back to the garage and I walked with Mom and Dad back to the house.

"Are you going to leave it there?" I asked.

"I don't know," Dad said. "You'd have to be very careful taking it out. You don't want to break the arrowhead or the shaft, which must be pretty delicate."

"How old do you think it is?" Mom asked him.

Dad sat down again in the living room and the boys joined us.

"Hard to tell," he said, thinking. "The tree is probably a hundred-seventy-five to two hundred years old. It probably would have been, say, thirty years old when the arrow hit it – before then, it wouldn't have been tall enough or thick enough."

He reached for a magazine and ballpoint and wrote some figures.

"Two hundred years would mean the tree was planted in 1762; thirty years after that would be 1792," he looked up to Mom. "That would be about when the house was supposed to have been built."

"The Indians had just left!" Dale laughed. "A parting shot!"

Mom and Dad laughed at this, but Steve and I didn't really get the joke.

"That would have been the earliest," Dad continued. "If the tree is only 175 years old, that means it would have been planted in 1787 and been thirty years old in 1817. So, the oldest it would be is a hundred-sixty."

"And the youngest?" Dale asked.

We looked at each other before Mom spoke.

"I can't see it being after the Civil War," she said.

"So, say, 1860," Dad said. "So it's at least a hundred

years old."

"But how likely is that?" Mom asked. "Wouldn't it have rotted or broken in all that time?"

Dad shook his head.

"I don't know," he said. "I'm going in to the college on Monday. I'll see who knows about artifacts and Indians. See if I can get an opinion on whether we leave it there or take it out."

Mom would take the film to be developed on Monday, too, so until then, there wasn't much more we could do except look for more arrows, but even Dale was less certain about going too deep into the woods.

≈

While waiting for Dad to talk to someone at the college and for the pictures to come back, we filled the days in pretty much the same way. We were just uneasy enough about the arrow not to be too impatient and remained cautious about going anywhere near it, or too far from the house. In consequence, we spend a lot of time by the stream and pond. The water was pretty cold and there hadn't been time for Mom and Dad to check the depth and rake the bottom to be sure it wasn't full of glass and old tin cans, but we walked barefoot around the edges and in the stream and then sat in the mottled shade and listen to the sounds of the heat.

The heat. Living in New England we accept the wide variation of seasonal temperatures as normal. From minus-ten or more in the winter to ninety-five in the summer – with humidity that varies just as much – has shaped the life and buildings of the region. I have now come to accept the two weeks in August when sleep is nearly impossible as a normal part of living here, but as a child, you wonder if it will ever end.

The heat had been building and we were in that period of humid stillness, waiting for the break. It added to the tension of wanting to see the arrow close-up and learn more about it. Dale and Steve were known to make up stories about things, but they were silent about the arrow. I put it down to weather-induced indolence.

When the pictures finally came back, we helped Dad select a few to show to someone who knew about Indians. People at the college thought it should be taken out of the tree and displayed somehow. There was the suggestion of a newspaper story, but Mom and Dad stopped that idea saying they didn't want people traipsing all over our property.

Typical. My one chance to be famous.

We talked about how we should display the arrow if we got it out of the tree. Dale had the idea of simply hanging it on a long cord in one of the large empty spaces on the wall near the fireplace. Everyone thought this was a good idea, but I wasn't sure I wanted it in the house.

Mom made the idea more acceptable when she

suggested we braid some colored ribbons to hang it from, and we started talking about colors.

Dad told us he had found a cardboard tube and some tissue paper and that, when he took it down, we could have a look at it. He'd put it on the table on the porch where we could see it (but not touch it) over the weekend. Then, he'd wrap it and take it to the college. He said he'd take it down on Saturday if the weather was still good.

When Saturday morning came, it was another scorcher. Our appetites had diminished with the heat, but we ate some fruit and cereal. Even Dad had forgone his normal Saturday bacon and eggs and settled for some orange juice and a piece of toast.

We all wanted to go out and watch him when he was going to extract it from the tree, but he didn't want an audience to distract him in case he made a movement that would damage it. The humidity had been climbing with the temperature and almost any movement resulted in the sticky feeling that made even turning the pages of a magazine unpleasant.

Mom tried to get him to put it off until it was cooler, but he wanted to be able to take the arrow to the college on Monday. There was a lot of stuff that Dad thought he needed and he let us help carry it out.

It took him a while to get ready with the ladder, a chisel, mallet, work gloves, and a small plank to lay it on once he extracted it. We'd think he had it all, but then he'd remember something else and we followed him back and forth a few times until he sent us inside and told us not to watch from the windows – not that we could see much. We heard him tapping the chisel, then it would be quiet, and then some more tapping. Each time he stopped, we expected him to walk in, but then it would start again.

Mom, Dale, Steve and I were chatting impatiently on the porch and tried to imagine what Dad was doing when we were startled by a sudden bright flash followed almost instantly with a crash of thunder that shook the house. Mom jumped up to be sure that Dad hadn't been struck by lightning, but he was entering the house carrying the arrow on the wooden plank as the heavens opened and torrential rain began to fall.

As the wind picked up, we ran around closing doors and windows. Dale, Steve and I ran upstairs to check up there. When I came down, ahead of the boys, I heard Mom and Dad talking softly in the dining room.

"I was terrified that you'd been struck," Mom was saying.

Dad was quiet for a moment, then said:

"The second I pulled that arrow out of the tree, the lightning flashed. I was so startled, I nearly dropped it."

He laughed a little.

"Don't worry. We're not in an episode of *The Twilight*

Zone."

I wasn't allowed to watch *The Twilight Zone*, but Dale would tell Steve and me the stories which was somehow more scary than the episodes when I eventually saw them.

I went into the kitchen to join the boys when they came down so Mom and Dad didn't suspect I'd overheard them.

"I was going to clean up the cuts on the tree and paint it and put the tools away," he said, watching the rain. "This won't last long.

"If you guys can get a tape measure, a pencil, some paper and the good magnifying glass," he continued, turning to us, "we'll take a good look at what we've got. I'll get the camera."

He started out of the room then turned back.

"Don't even think about touching it," he said.

He didn't say it loudly, but it was his most serious voice, and he knew we wouldn't.

We gathered around to have a closer look before Dale told us to get the stuff Dad had asked for.

We foraged for the things together and when we got back to the porch we found Mom with a big bag of her rug-braiding material and a pair of scissors.

"While waiting for your father, why don't you look through the bag and select colors that would make a good cord to hang it from," she said. "Choose three."

Thoughts and Whispers

"Aren't these too thick?" Steve asked.

We had all seen Mom braid rugs while we watched television on the weekends. During the week, she was ironing or darning.

"That's why I brought the scissors," she said. "I can cut each length into two or three strips. We don't want it too thick, but thick enough so people can see the colors."

We took a few handfuls of material out of the bag and began sorting through it.

We were arguing about colors when Dad re-appeared.

"What can you tell me about it?" he asked.

We couldn't tell him much, having been effectively distracted by Mom.

"We've chosen two colors," I said. "This dark orange and this dark gray. We just need one more."

"I like the dark green," Steve said, but "Dale likes the dark red."

We laid out the colors for him to see.

"Try the orange, green and red," he suggested.

We debated this until Mom intervened.

"Why don't I braid a short length and you can see what it looks like."

She did that while the rest of us crowded over the arrow. Dad picked up the large magnifying glass.

"I'm not going to pretend that I know anything

about this," he said. "I can tell you that the arrowhead is stuck into a notch in the shaft that's tied with something and then stuck with something. I don't know what wood the shaft is. It wouldn't have made a difference as long as it was straight. But here, at the end, you can see a few bits of the feather fletching left. It's been stuck with something and the leading edges look like its tied, though there's a lot of gunk on them."

"Bird poop," I said, and everyone laughed at me.

"Well, in two hundred years, a bird is bound to have pooped on it!" I protested, but the laughter only grew louder until Mom hugged me and told me it wasn't what I said, but the way I'd said it.

I seemed to say a lot of things funny.

"What tribe is this from?" Dale asked.

"I have no idea," Dad said.

"You're *supposed* to be an historian," Mom teased him.

"Not my period," he said with a laugh. "Bob will know, or Peter."

We all had a look at the arrow through the magnifying glass and when we'd done, Mom showed us two sample cords made from the different colors.

I think she was expecting a big argument from us, but all of us chose the orange, green and red. It just looked right.

It was still raining after lunch when Mom and I sat

on the porch braiding the material. The boys were watching the ball game. The Red Sox were playing somewhere dry. We'd measured the arrow and thought that making what Mom called an equilateral triangle with it would look good, which gave us a long braid to make.

"How are we going to attach it to the arrow?" I asked.

"We can make some loops, or Daddy might find some rings or hooks we can use," Mom said.

The rain stopped around supper time, so afterwards Dad went out and brought the ladder and tools in and wiped them down. It was a little bit cooler, but it was still humid.

∽

The last week of summer vacation was already here. With the slightly cooler weather, we wanted to make the most of our time and, apart from playing on our own, we explored a little farther than we had before.

Dad had taken the arrow to his friends in the history department and were examining it. We were disappointed that there was no news when he came home Monday afternoon, and had mixed feelings when he told us that we'd have to wait for the weekend.

"Dr. Flynn, Peter, told me that a museum had just opened about the Nipmuc Indian tribe and culture. It's in Grafton, and he and I will go there Saturday and take the arrow with us and see if they can tell us anything."

"Did your colleagues have anything they could tell you?" Mom asked him.

He laughed.

"Nothing definite: it could be this, it could be that," he said. "There's a good chance that this isn't a Nipmuc arrow, as we are on the fringe of their area. It might be Nashua, but those two tribes were the only ones likely to be here.

"Someone wondered if it was from the King Philip Wars, but they ended in 1678 and our tree is far too young for that," Dad went on. "There's nothing anyone could see that gave us clues, which is why taking it to the Nipmuc is a good idea."

"So you learned nothing," Dale said.

Dad smiled.

"We learned a few things," he replied. "We took it to the science labs. The wood is probably elm, and the arrowhead is quartzite, which is why it has a bit of color showing. They also thought it was pine pitch that was sticking on the feathers. The small cords are apt to be animal hide or sinews, covered in pitch – which is why it's lasted so long."

We thought about this and Dale and Steve talked about how difficult it would be to make one.

"The first few would take quite a while," Dad said. "But, hundreds were needed, so you'd eventually get good at making them and do one in about half an hour."

"Including chipping the head?" Dale asked.

"That's right," Dad replied. "You'd be good at selecting the right stone, and would have cut pieces to a rough size before starting. Then you'd finish it with pressure flaking, rather than hitting it with something. It takes a lot of skill."

Over the next few days, Dad brought home two old-looking black metal pieces to hang the arrow from.

"They're open, like a hook now," he explained to Steve and me, "but when we rest the arrow in it, we can close up the opening so it's like a figure-eight. We need to close the loop because the arrow head will be heavier than the end with the feathers and it will help hold it straight."

Mom took the hooks and looked at them, and said that she'd sew them to the end of the braided cord so they looked neat.

As the week went on, the plans to go to Grafton became more clear. Not only would Dr. Flynn go with Dad, but so would Dr. Robins (Bob). They would then come over later for an end-of-summer cookout and we'd hang the arrow. (Dad had found an old hand-forged nail that looked like a big horseshoe nail in the garage and thought it would look better than a modern nail or a brass picture hook.)

It seemed to be taking forever, but I liked the way things were coming together, and looked forward to the news from the museum. Mom and I were getting things ready for the start of school. New clothes, a compass of my own for drawing circles, some new colored pencils and new shoes. I'd spent the summer in sneakers outside and flip-flops inside. We went shopping and had lunch together and I was feeling more grown up.

Mom did a similar trip with Dale and Steve, and because it was raining, she took them bowling. I later learned that this was in exchange for their agreement to be helpful on Saturday getting ready for the cookout and during the evening itself.

Dad set out early Saturday morning to pick up his colleagues and drive to Grafton. They'd have breakfast on the way and take their time. The rest of us were getting ready for the evening, sweeping the porch, moving the grill out, getting the charcoal, lighter, tongs and other things with long handles together. Mom wanted to rearrange the furniture on the porch and also set up some chairs on the lawn not too far from the grill. She said that Dad had a list of things to pick up on the way back.

It was about two o'clock when Dad got home carrying the tube with the arrow and the shopping bags. We rushed to him and started firing questions.

"Let Daddy catch his breath," Mom said, greeting him. "Have a wash and go sit on the porch, I'll bring you some iced tea."

We all lined up on the swing, and Dad sat in one of the comfortable chairs. Mom had an iced tea, too, and sat back to listen to what he had to say.

"I can't tell you much," he began, "but what I learned was interesting. As you will come to appreciate, three historians can ask more questions than three children, and John, who is a curator and a member of the tribe who knows about Indian artifacts, told us about the Nipmuc Indians and the Hassanamisco Reservation."

"You were on an Indian reservation?" Steve asked excitedly.

"Yes, I was. It's not very big, only a few acres, but the land has never belonged to any white man; it's always belonged to the Nipmucs," Dad explained. "The tribe is now headed by Zara Cisco Brough, better known as Princess White Flower."

"Princess!?" Steve and I said simultaneously.

Dad laughed.

"Yes. We didn't meet her today, but Bob and Peter are going to invite her to speak at the college," he said.

"What about the arrow?" Dale asked.

"Yeah!"

Dad opened his hands.

"The people at the museum were fascinated by the story, the arrow and the photographs," he began. "John confirmed what I told you about the head being quartzite and the shaft possibly being elm. He also said that it would have been pine pitch that was used to help secure the head and the feathers, and that thin strips of leather and sinews were used to tie them."

"Nothing new?" Steve asked, disappointed with the report so far.

"I'm afraid not," Dad said sympathetically. "He told us that there is really no way to tell one tribe's arrow from another's except by making a guess based on the stone of the arrow head or the bird the feathers came from. You might be able to scientifically discover what bird the feathers came from, but even that won't tell you much if it was a pigeon, quail, pheasant, duck, goose or turkey – all of which were likely.

"Quartzite is common around here, he said, but he didn't know if it was one of theirs or a Nashua arrow. Unless it was an uncommon stone or an unusual bird, the arrow could have been from virtually any tribe in the country."

"We're you disappointed about driving all that way?" Mom asked.

Dad laughed.

"Not at all. The history department was very pleased to find that their surmises were correct," he said. "It's always good to have some validation."

"No guesses on age, then?" Mom asked again.

Dad shook his head.

"I explained how we'd formulated our guess, and

they reckoned that was a sound estimate. I did ask a question we hadn't talked about: how was it that there were trees in a field that had been cleared?"

Dad looked at us.

"Any of you think of that?"

We shook our heads.

"John said he didn't think that was unusual, particularly if the tree was a decent size when the field was cleared. He said that because the field was near the house, it may have had animals in it, to minimize the distance water had to be carried and just general checking. Good trees would also provide a bit of shade for cows, horses and pigs during the summer. If they were oak trees, the pigs could eat the acorns, but oak trees didn't mean there were necessarily pigs there."

That evening, when the guests were there and everyone had heard the story and had a good look at the arrow, we went into the living room and Dad banged the nail in, pinched the rings shut and began to hang the arrow, but before he put it up, Mom stopped him. He looked surprised and turned around.

Mom laughed.

"I didn't mean to startle you," she said. "I just wondered which direction it should point. What does everyone think?"

We looked at the guests who didn't immediately speak, but Dale, Steve and I said, almost at once,

"Towards the fireplace." The guests echoed that decision, so Dad turned it and reached up and hung it on the nail. He stepped back to look and made a final adjustment to level the shaft.

The colors of the cord against the wall and the color of the arrowhead looked really great. People took time to look closely, as it was hanging at adult eye level, and were fascinated by its age and the circumstances in which it was found.

We didn't think any more about it as our new school year began and we were busy with school activities, new friends and, for the boys, homework. We didn't do much together on Saturday, but after supper we were watching television in the living room when Dad came in, stood watching with us for a minute, then suddenly went up to the TV and switched it off.

"Hey, Dad! What's that for?" Steve complained loudly.

"I want to know which one of you did that," he said, raising his head towards the fireplace.

We looked over our shoulders.

"Did what?" Dale asked.

"Just look," Dad said. He sounded cross.

We looked back and forth blankly.

"Look at what?" Dale dared to ask again.

"I told you not to touch that arrow. It's old and very delicate."

We turned around and looked. No one said anything because they didn't notice at first. I did.

"It's pointing towards the window!" I exclaimed.

"I'd like to know who moved it," Dad repeated.

We looked at each other. I was pretty good at telling who was lying. Dale and Steve didn't lie much, only when they were teasing me, which I am glad to say, wasn't often. They were more apt to ignore me. I knew *I* didn't do it.

Dad moved to the door.

"Pat, can you come in here a minute," he called.

When she came in, he pointed at the arrow. It took her a moment to notice it wasn't pointing the way it had been.

"You didn't change it, did you?"

"No. I thought it looked great the way it was. Does it matter?" she said.

"It only matters if one of your children did it and isn't owning up to it."

That was one of Dad's things. We were *her* children when we were misbehaving. At least when he was speaking. When *she* had discovered something we'd done, we were *his* children.

"Nothing's going to happen," Mom said reassuringly. "Just tell us."

It was then I got scared, put my head down, and couldn't stop tears coming out.

"Boys, go play outside or upstairs while Mom and I talk to Molly."

Of course, that made me cry louder.

"How could she have done that?" Mom asked. "That nail is way too high for her to reach."

I looked up to indicate that she was right: I couldn't have done it.

"Why are you crying, then?" Dad asked. He tried to sound gentle, but I could tell he was still irritated with me.

Mom gave me a tissue which gave me time to think.

"I didn't do it," I said calmly and evenly, but feeling like I was going to start shaking. "I'm crying because I'm scared."

"What have you got to be scared of?" Mom asked.

She *did* sound gentle.

"I know I didn't do it, and I can tell that Dale and Steve didn't do it either," I said, just about controlling my voice.

"So who did?" Dad asked, very softly.

"That's why I'm scared!"

Dad held me, not saying much, until Mom took me upstairs and gave me a bubble bath. We went to my room and she read me one of my favorite stories, and I fell asleep before she'd finished.

In the morning, Dale and Steve were acting normally. When we went in to breakfast, Mom told us that Dad had moved the arrow back to pointing to the fireplace, so not to be bothered when we saw it. She said no more about it and made pancakes.

Our week was busy with school and other activities and things were feeling happy and normal. The boys teased each other and me; they played games in the afternoons and evenings on the lawn, and we walked to the pond several times. We also checked the tree to see how Dad had cleaned it up after removing the arrow. He'd actually done a pretty good job. The knobbly bits had been cut back and tidied up and it was now neatly sealed with thick black paint. From a distance, you could hardly see it.

Making new friends at school was okay. I was missing my old ones, but there were a few girls here that were nice and we were starting to spend more time together. Mom said that when I moved to junior high, these people would all be old friends and make the rest of school much easier. I think she knew I was still feeling lost.

Since the weather was still hot, we were practically living on the porch. Dale was even doing his homework there. It was nice because at about seven-thirty each evening a breeze would blow across the porch. It wasn't strong, but it relieved the stillness and dropped the temperature by a few degrees. You could almost feel all of us relax a little when we felt it. It helped to cool the bedrooms and made sleeping easier.

"Somehow, people knew just where to build houses," Dad said.

He was right. The house was near a hill that could protect it, and it had a wonderful view from the porch that looked over an ocean of trees without a building in sight. I was snuggling contentedly into the scatter cushions on the swing when Steve suddenly shouted from the other room.

"Dad! Dad! Come here!"

We all rushed off the porch into the living room. We thought he'd injured himself even though we hadn't heard anything.

We found him staring at the wall.

The arrow was pointing out the window.

Dad turned to all of us.

"This isn't funny," he said, about as angry as I'd seen him. "Does anyone have anything to say?"

We started by shaking our heads as he looked at each of us. Then Dale spoke.

"I did not touch that arrow, Dad," he said. He was very serious and no one had any reason to doubt him. My brothers, pains that they could be, usually owned up to anything they'd done. I spoke next and repeated what Dale had said and added, "And I couldn't reach the nail anyway."

Steve also repeated it. His voice was still shaky which

made him sound doubly convincing.

We stared at each other and the arrow for nearly a full minute, then Mom spoke:

"That's it. I want it out of here!"

She sounded forceful and determined. There would be no arguing about it.

"Leave it the way it is, then on Monday, take it to the college then drive it to the museum as soon as possible. I'm sure Princes White Flower would love to have it."

And that was it.

The arrow stayed, pointing at the window for the rest of the weekend, then Dad wrapped it as before and took it to the college. Dr. Flynn had arranged for Princess White Flower to come to speak a few weeks later, and it was presented to her on that visit.

Mom eventually found an old picture at an antique shop to occupy the space, and it stayed facing the right direction.

The incident wasn't talked about beyond those who had been there when it was first hung. Once it was out of the house, all we said to each other was that it was strange, but then it receded in our memories, displaced by our increasingly active lives in Westbury.

I made friends; Steve made the swimming team; Dale got a girlfriend. Mom and Dad continued to work on the farm, garden and land around the house. By the time summer came around again, we had seen the double apple tree bloom at different times in the spring and in different colors, and we were looking forward to a summer of cookouts, having our new friends around and showing them our favorite places in the woods.

It was during our Fourth of July cookout that we heard Steve calling us from the back of the house. Only taking time to remove the London Broil from the barbecue, we raced around the building. Dad's colleagues Dr. Flynn and Dr. Robins were there with their wives (or whatever) and we ran into the wooded field where Steve stood by the wall staring at the tree.

Mom put her arms around him, while Dad, Bob and Peter moved in close to inspect.

An arrow was stuck about three-quarters of an inch into the trunk. It had another quartzite arrowhead, a full complement of fletches, and the wood of the shaft was green.

Thoughts and Whispers

Dark Lady

Thoughts and Whispers

Dark Lady

July 1974

I was taking a visiting friend through Highgate Cemetery one hot afternoon, shortly before it looked as though that graveyard would close its gates forever, when I saw the figure of a woman passing between the trees nearby.

It startled me because the hot stillness had combined with Highgate's peculiar atmosphere and made me a little nervous. I peered round the trees to see the woman – mostly to ensure that her feet were, in fact, touching the ground. She was dressed completely in black: long black skirt, full black blouse with lace, black gloves, a small black parasol; black buttoned shoes and stockings and a large black hat, trimmed with a veil and a black ostrich feather.

She didn't look around, but I did see her face for a moment. She looked as though she had stepped from a Pre-Raphaelite painting: perfectly made up, with her reddish-brown hair pulled back and tied somewhere under her hat.

It was a romantic vision and I watched her for as long as I could as she headed for the northwest corner of the cemetery and was lost behind a great elm. I confess to conferring with my visitor to confirm that we had both seen her.

In previous visits to Highgate, I had seen some odd people. One couple occupied themselves collecting four-leaf clover for their eighteen-month old son, carefully recording each find in a small loose-leaf notebook. (For some reason, a great number grow near canals, I was told.) Then, there was the man shredding an entire loaf of bread and tossing the bits on to the path for the birds – only there weren't any birds. It was also widely reported that a man was found hiding in the overgrowth with a leather bag containing a mallet and several wooden stakes.

One comes to forgive London for such things.

When I recalled my dark lady in more mundane surroundings, she seemed blatantly theatrical: the scene was right for the time and place, but the effect could not be sustained beyond that. Still, what prompted an attractive girl to dress like that and traipse through cemeteries? Not finding an intriguing answer, I forgot about her.

It must have been six weeks later while in Hampstead (looking for second-hand books) that I saw her again. She was dressed in exactly the same costume and sat, alone, at a table in Louis' patisserie. I saw her a fortnight later on the heath, wandering among the trees and through the tall grass. But, the sighting which most affected me was the third one, when I came unexpectedly face to face with her in a second-hand music shop. She startled me by suddenly appearing from behind a case of miniature scores. Our eyes met; she may have begun to smile.

Curiosity finally over-powered me. When she had left the shop, I asked the shopkeeper if he knew her. Musicians, unlike other artists, are willing to be sociable; perhaps it is because music can be produced collectively, unlike paintings or books which require solitude.

The shopkeeper, who knew me only as an account holder, told me that she had picked up some music for the pianist Erich Proust Gaunt.

That was the first thing which made sense about her. About that time, Gaunt was making a name for himself as a very talented, if eccentric, pianist with outspoken opinions on the arts and philosophy. My dark lady fit into his world perfectly, as Gaunt was in the habit of imitating the nineteenth century composer–pianists, and frequently dressed in the more flamboyant Victorian manner.

I was not unashamedly intrigued; curious; all right, nosy. One of my friends lived in the same building as Gaunt.

Richard was enormously amused when I rang him up.

"You want to see me so that you can meet Gaunt and

thereby meet this Vision in Black whom you've fallen for!"

I explained that I hadn't fallen for her, but I don't think I sounded convincing.

Richard suggested that we go to a concert where Gaunt was playing or likely to attend. With luck, the girl would be there, too.

Erich Proust ("pronounced to rhyme with Faust, Gaunt would say) Gaunt began drawing attention at the Royal College of Music. He had given several recitals which attracted critical notice. His appearance was always theatrical in an undergraduate sort of way, but his playing was good enough to get away with it.

He began performing his own compositions and announced his intention of reviving the tradition of the composer-virtuoso. Gaunt did this premiering a sonata when he was twenty-two and a collection of etudes a year later. He was reported to be at work on a concerto, but he would never speak publicly about his unfinished works.

Richard and I went to a recital two weeks later on Sunday afternoon. It was crowded and our seats weren't particularly good. We could see much piano and very little pianist.

He played a varied programme of Liszt, Busoni, Rachmaninoff and Bartok. For an encore, justly deserved, he played one of his own études. Although I scanned the auditorium during the performance and in the interval, I could not see the dark lady anywhere.

When Gaunt finished the étude, we made our way to the Green Room where there was a crush of teenage piano students; the boys in obvious admiration of Gaunt's talent; the girls in frenzied raving. Gaunt chatted to all of them, said the right things and signed flamboyant autographs.

It was no wonder that the girls flocked to his concerts. He was very tall, slim and dark. He had high cheekbones and deep-set eyes, which made his looks live up to his name. In his white tie and tails (even on Sunday afternoon) he looked as though he belonged on a film set.

When Richard and I were near him in the queue, he noticed Richard and gave a smile and a nod. When we reached him, he was charming, though his manner reflected his theatrical appearance.

"Richard, how good of you to come," he said with a flourish. "It's not often one's friends come to these things."

I was introduced.

"You'd think being a concert pianist would impress one's friends. Well, I might as well be a bus conductor: 'How was work today? More of the usual?' 'Yes; three curtain calls, one encore; the symphony played well, nine hundred twenty-three in the hall.' We all have our work."

"Do you suppose you could get a few hours off to come for a drink?" Richard asked.

"Tonight?"

"Yes. Come tell us how the bus route's been."

"Love to. Eight o'clock?"

"We're going out, Erich," a voice said softly beside us.

We all looked. There she was, just as she'd been when I first saw her. It was a look that later became known as Goth, though on closer inspection, it was more a re-enactor's costume.

"We can go some other time," Gaunt said to her, gently but decisively.

"Erich, you promised," she said, only half daring to protest.

"No, my dear. I believe that a quiet evening with friends is the best for tonight. I'm tired and fancy a homely evening."

"Perhaps you could join us," Richard said to her.

"I hardly – "

Erich introduced us. We weren't given her last name, but her first name was Melinda.

On the way back to the flat, Richard admitted that she was stunning, and conceded that to have seen her drift through an over-grown cemetery must have been a captivating and disconcerting sight.

We waited impatiently at the flat to see whether she

would come or not. Gaunt might feel that it was a gentleman's evening and not bring her; or she might be miffed enough not to join him.

A few minutes after eight, Gaunt arrived, Melinda with him. He looked around the flat and decided it looked comfortable. He unashamedly opened the lid of the stereo to see who was performing. It was not Erich Proust Gaunt. Richard and I had debated whether or not to play one of his records.

"No objection to Weissenberg from me," he said. "He plays Rachmaninoff beautifully – if the word 'beautiful' may be applied to Rachmaninoff at all."

Richard began to protest.

"'Beautiful' is a feminine adjective. Rachmaninoff is never feminine."

"Point taken."

I felt that if we didn't get Melinda to talk soon, she would fade away completely. Already, she had seated herself in a straight chair, away from us, and listened intently to the record.

"Dry, medium or sweet?" I asked her.

"Amontillado, if you have it, please. This is my favourite prelude," she said quietly.

"The B-flat minor? It's not a very popular one. The C-sharp minor and the G are always the ones requested and played."

"Rachmaninoff came to hate the C-sharp minor.

When people asked what moved him to write it, he'd answer, 'Forty roubles,' – one twenty-fourth the commission of the whole set."

Gaunt spoke with pleasing theatricality, but he sounded personal at the same time. Often when speaking with people, he'd use their names, even if he'd just met them in a backstage crush.

He presented an uncomfortable combination of contact and intensity.

"I believe that to listen to music in complete silence is one of the greatest luxuries there is. So often people treat it as background, or even worse, mere noise to drown out background noise."

"I'm afraid I'm guilty of that," I said. "At university, after playing squash, I used to put on *Elektra* and fall asleep. It drowned out all the noise."

"Philistine!" Gaunt said, but not with malice.

We chatted for three hours, during which Melinda was silent except for an occasional word of agreement with whatever Gaunt had said. When I finally succeeded in engaging her in a discussion, Gaunt announced that it was time to go, and they went.

Apart from finding out that part of her name was Melinda, I had learned nothing. Why did she dress that way? What did she do? Who was she?

A month later after lunch with friends at the Flask, I decided to go through Highgate Cemetery a last time, for now news of its closure was about, and there was even talk of building flats on the land, which would be doomed to be haunted.

I walked from the Rotunda past Mrs Henry Wood to the northwest corner where I had first seen Melinda. I walked behind the elm tree and scanned the stones. Two were pressed against each other, the lettering barely legible. One was Christina Rossetti's, the other belonged to her sister-in-law, Elizabeth Siddal Rossetti.

I tried to imagine that night in 1848 when Mrs Rossetti was exhumed and her husband took from beneath her long red tresses the volume of his poems which he had placed there seven years previously. Would any of that famous hair still be there?

"Poor Guggums. Just like me," a voice said behind me. It was Melinda.

"We won't be able to visit her much longer," she said.

"Where will they put her? What will they do with all these people. Over a hundred thousand of them. And the animals, the birds, squirrels, rabbits and fox?" she asked in a dreamy way.

"You startled me," I said.

"How terrible they were to her," she went on. "What did she ever do to them? They never stopped. Paint, paint, paint. It killed her."

There were tears in her eyes.

"Melinda, that was over a hundred years ago."

"People still have that power. They can kill just as effectively, and *never* get caught. She knew what they were doing, too, but she must have thought it was worth it; after all, it bought her immortality of a sort."

I couldn't follow what she was saying, so I offered to buy her tea. Her mood changed almost instantly we left the cemetery.

At tea, we chatted about Gaunt, his playing, his music and music generally. She tricked me into doing most of the talking so that when we finished, I had only one new piece of information: her surname was Marlowe.

"Gaunt and I are giving a dinner party on the twenty-third. Please come. Eight-thirty."

"I'll be there. Will there be music?"

"There's *always* music," she said wearily. "Just as with Guggums, there was only paint." She paused, then added softly: "'Dead wood more blest than living lips.'"

☙

A week later, I received a more formal invitation to Gaunt's party. I called Richard to see if he had got one as well. He hadn't, but he would be away in any case.

"Have fun, though," he said. "I expect Erich will be far different from the person you met after the recital. He's a different man in his own surroundings. Cheers."

Although Gaunt's flat was in the same building as Richard's, it was nothing at all like it. Where Richard's was bright, cheerful and modern, Gaunt's was dark, heavy and Victorian. There were lush oriental rugs on the floors, large European antique furniture and ornaments. A grand piano dominated the sitting room.

The walls provided a shocking contrast to the rest of the room. They were decorated with very large abstract paintings in various different styles and tones, dominantly red, purple and black. The effect was startling. There were about a dozen people there when I arrived. Gaunt met me at the door and Melinda was just behind him carrying a silver tray with glasses of sherry.

"How good of you to come!" Gaunt said in his mannered way but enthusiastically.

"It was nice of you to include me," I said, already sensing that this was not my kind of party. It was an affluent, influential and arty crowd. I recognised, among others, an antique dealer, a painter and, surprisingly, a music critic. There was no one I knew. After looking at all the furniture, studying the book titles and inspecting the paintings, I began to watch Melinda. She still carried the silver tray and made small talk with different guests as she gave them drinks.

Her black dress was far less out of place at a party than in public. She wore her hair up, tied in black velvet cords which hung down her neck. A choker of what looked like black pearls smouldered at her throat. She wore black nail varnish and a silver ring set with a jet the size of a walnut. Only the sherry she carried broke the unity of tone.

Word eventually was passed for dinner. Doors to an elegant dining room were thrown open and a long table, flanked by high-backed, upholstered chairs seized the attention of everyone. Each place was set to the limit with crystal glasses, Royal Worcester, and silver.

I was seated on Melinda's right, several places away from Gaunt.

"I'm afraid I'm being boring," I said to Melinda. "I don't know anyone here."

"You'll know soon enough if you're boring. You won't be invited again if he thinks you are. I don't know anyone here either."

"That's hard to believe."

"No one is paying attention to me. I'm just a prop. Sometimes I wonder if Gaunt knows me. She paused, then added, "He does, though. Too well."

I didn't think that line of conversation was going to lead anywhere but was unable to think of a suitable alternative.

"The pictures in the sitting room – " I began.

"Erich's. He paints brilliantly, too. There's a portrait in the bedroom. I'll sneak you in to see it if there's a chance."

"A portrait of?"

"Me. Immortalised by Erich Proust Gaunt. It's me in

so many ways. I hate it."

"Like Dorian Gray?"

"No! Not at all like that," she said quickly. "It's a good likeness."

She was now uneasy and I felt I had lost my chance of seeing it now.

I turned from Melinda to listen to Gaunt who was practically addressing the entire table. He talked of some coming recital and suggested that we all come to it. When he had finished, I turned back to Melinda.

"It'll be a good one," she said. "They nearly all are."

She wasn't sounding like a friend – if she ever was a friend – but like the prop to which she had referred.

After dinner, Gaunt gave a short recital. He played some short Mozart and Beethoven pieces, then changed the mood and played Liszt and Prokofiev. When he finished, several friends asked him to play an original work.

"I am now at work on a new piece," he said. "It's a toccata and fantasia which I hope to have finished in another month or so. However, I shan't play it until it's finished."

There were a few expressions of disappointment which Gaunt waved off. He then sat down and thundered out a powerful Chopinesque waltz which was haunting and compelling.

Later, over brandy, someone asked about the haunted

quality of some music.

"Much of it is a question of obsession. I do not hold with the theory of aesthetic qualities arising from non-aesthetic ones," Gaunt said. "Chopin and Poland, or Georges Sand; Berlioz and his Henrietta, or even Estelle; it's obsession with something – usually a woman – that stimulates the opus."

A rude remark was made at this point.

"It's as though the muse were essential to the creative artist – a *familiar*, if you will. He'd attach himself to her and suck out every bit of feeling, emotion, spirit, *angst* or whatever, until there was nothing left.

"Again, consider Berlioz: he pursued Henrietta Smithson for years; wrote her theme into everything – all five movements of the *Symphonie Phantastique* – then when he finally persuaded her to marry him, what happens? They're miserable together! Why? Because he has sucked her dry of inspiration. She could no longer fulfil his creative needs, her spirit is on paper, in music."

Gaunt was gathering momentum as he spoke. He was obviously on a pet topic, but one which captivated his guests. Only Melinda looked disenchanted with the forceful digression.

Gaunt continued.

"Art itself is destructive. When the inspiration comes from within, it's suicide. The spirit burns itself out in the transmigration from the spiritual to the worldly. I need only remind you of E. M. Forster who wrote seven novels before 1926 and none ever again. He dried up, burnt himself out.

"Do you know why Schubert's eighth symphony is unfinished? It was too good – a clear case of over-achievement. Had he finished it, it would have finished him. He had to stop composing it to ensure his survival.

"If one has external inspiration, the life is sucked from that. Is that, then, murder? But just as some African tribes fear the camera, lest it steal their souls, so should the rest of the world fear the creative artist, for he can capture their lives:

And all should cry, Beware! Beware!
His flashing eyes, his floating hair!
Weave a circle round him thrice,
And close your eyes in holy dread,
For he on honeydew hath fed,
And drunk the milk of Paradise!"

Undergraduate nonsense that it was, it was entertaining, and Gaunt *could* paint and play. I kept my thoughts to myself and enjoyed the questions raised by the others. Maybe it was politeness – or even fear – but none seriously challenged him.

"Aren't you confusing Paradise with parasites?" someone asked, provoking a short laugh.

"Doesn't everyone?"

"But surely not vampirism?"

"Not literally, but certainly intellectually, emotionally. Artists die when they have traded their entire being for completed canvases, a stack of books or a number of symphonies. It's rubbish to say, 'Oh, what he could have done had he lived.' The very reason that he did die was because he could do no more. He had wrung all the vitality from himself.

"This is only true of geniuses. There are excellent craftsmen who will paint good, but uninspired, pictures for decades, or compose dozens of major works. But a true genius cannot sustain uncompromised production," he said.

Before anyone could challenge the use of "genius," Gaunt continued.

"Why do you think the phrase 'suck the life out of someone' is so prevalent and enduring?" he demanded.

"Can someone be killed with notes on a page, or paint or words?" someone ventured.

"Yes! If they were a complete reflection of the spirit. Life could be drained – either from oneself or from some external source of inspiration."

At this point, the room was sharply divided between those ready to accept Gaunt's thesis, and those who thought this was utter pseudo-intellectual rubbish.

Gaunt didn't stop. He went on bludgeoning us with examples.

"Why did Lizzie Siddal Rossetti die so young?"

No one suggested that she died of an overdose of laudanum.

"Because Millais, Rossetti and the others literally painted her to death! Certainly, she nearly drowned while Millais painted Ophelia, but she didn't. She killed herself when she knew she was only a shell of what she was. A husk to be discarded. How many artists and writers have killed themselves this century? Dozens! Hundreds! Because they are empty!"

Gaunt's argument was not wholly original, but in the context of his Victorian gothic flat, and his compelling manner, it made for an unnerving evening. He used lang-uage brilliantly to suit his purposes.

Some of the guests looked in a state resembling fear when he returned to the keyboard.

He played the Rachmaninoff B-flat minor prelude, and there were tears on Melinda's cheeks.

After that evening, I did not hear from Gaunt again.

I had been a boring guest.

Richard, however, heard from him and attended an evening similar to the one where I had failed to distinguish myself. The only difference was, on this occasion, Gaunt played a part of his new Toccata and Fantasia. According to Richard, it was brilliant.

∞

A couple of years passed and life moved on. I had had no contact with Erich Gaunt, nor with Richard.

However, Richard had been a friend since university, so I was not surprised when he telephoned me one afternoon and asked if I could come round as soon as possible.

I reached his flat at tea time and could hear piano music thundering in the stairwells. Gaunt was clearly still in residence.

Richard looked distraught when he answered the door.

"Thank God you're here. You've got to explain it all to him. He's going to do something drastic," he blurted.

Richard shut the door swiftly and I followed him through the hall into the sitting room. I stopped in the doorway and stared.

On the opposite wall was a very large painting. It was Gaunt's portrait of Melinda.

In the opposite corner was a woman wearing a tweed skirt and white jumper with long hair pulled up and loosely tied. It took a moment to realise that this was Melinda herself.

I'd never seen her in normal clothes before, yet even without her Victorian mourning and exaggerated make-up, she still looked unhealthy. I glanced at her face and the pallid flesh tones of the portrait. If anything she looked more pale and was certainly thinner.

I was still trying to take all this in when she spoke.

"Is he going to help?" Melinda asked Richard

anxiously.

"Yes, darling. It will be all right."

This, of course, was news to me.

They exchanged looks and I felt that it was one of those circumstances where one is better off knowing as little as possible for as long as possible.

"I don't know how much you know about things," Richard began. "When was the last time you saw Gaunt?"

"At the dinner party. Two years ago."

He nodded.

"You knew I went to a party there not long afterwards?"

"Yes."

"Well, while Gaunt was going on after dinner about his usual artistic nonsense and captivating the social-climbing parasites, Melinda and I were having our own little *tête a tête*. She showed me the portrait," he waved towards it.

"It's beautiful, isn't it? Why do men like Gaunt hoard beauty? He has his music, why does he need pictures and Melinda as well? Do you know how miserable her life with him was? The constant threat, the hate, the fear?"

I let the question remain rhetorical.

"She was ignored completely."

He paused.

"After that evening, Melinda began coming here

while Gaunt was playing and stopped going to his concerts and recitals and spent the time with me."

"That," Richard continued, "was when the real hate campaign began. There was a rather unpleasant scene when he charged in here one evening and demanded that she come back at once. She refused and I asked him to leave. The next morning, all her things were dumped on the pavement outside the building. There were a few pieces of rather good jewellery missing which I went to ask him for."

He took a breath.

"It didn't get me anywhere. Gaunt said that when Melinda first came to him, she had nothing; that he had given her everything. He was keeping the jewellery but had no use for the dresses.

"Then, he asked me to leave. Since he had left my flat without protest when I asked him to, I really had no choice."

Richard said the last by way of apology.

"There was nearly three hundred pounds worth of jewellery there," Melinda said with a spite in her voice I had not heard before.

"It was time for positive action," Richard said. "One night while Gaunt was giving a recital, I went into his flat to recover the jewellery. It wasn't there, or I couldn't find it. So, I took the portrait."

"I'm surprised he didn't have the police on you," I

said.

"It is my portrait," Melinda said. "He gave it to me."

"At the moment, Gaunt can't afford adverse publicity. His recent reviews have been indifferent and the critics are waiting to finish him off. Anything in the papers would look like a publicity stunt, which is cheap. You can't jeopardise a genius for a thing like that."

"We decided to keep this on our own level," Richard said. "There was a flurry of hate letters and dead animals left on doorsteps. Then there were more serious ones. Notes on milk bottles saying they'd been poisoned, and threats of damage to my car. The telephone would ring at all hours of the night, then the wires were cut. Then he wrote a scurrilous account of Melinda's past."

I thought it was all juvenile and embarrassing, but nothing more.

"Then there was this past week," Richard said. "That was the worst."

"What happened?"

"Absolutely nothing," said Melinda in a whisper.

"Can you imagine the tension?" Richard said. "Melinda was nearly out of her mind. Do you know what it is to be afraid to enter and leave your own home?"

"Erich said he'd have the last word," Melinda said. "He always does."

Richard drew an envelope from his pocket.

"This came this morning. It's two tickets to his

recital tonight. Something's wrong," Richard said. "I don't know what he's up to."

"I expect he's just tired of childish games," I said.

Melinda said nothing.

"Look, old man," Richard said. "I've bought an extra ticket. It's not in the box but fairly near the front. I want to foil his little plan, whatever it is."

"You're sure he's up to something?"

"Of course he is!"

"Then, don't go," I said.

"I want you to come tonight. You take the box with Melinda, and I'll be in the stalls. He won't see me there and he'll also know I'm not where he wants me to be."

It was pointless to argue. I didn't believe a word of this melodrama, and the concert would be good.

The recital was in a hall that had long been closed, and new owners were trying to stimulate its revival. The acoustics were meant to be excellent, but the paint was peeling from every surface and only some hastily nailed-together flats screened the back wall.

Melinda and I found our way to the box and watched as the audience took their places.

"It looks like a full house," I said to Melinda.

"It always is."

Richard didn't go to his seat until the lights were ready to go down. He insisted that I stay out of sight, too. Melinda occupied the box, dressed modestly (and modernly) in black. I waited behind the curtain to the box until Gaunt was seated, then slipped into my chair, thinking that Richard had seen too many reruns of *The Phantom of the Opera.*

Gaunt looked his usual self, tall, dark and somewhat brutal looking as he prepared to bring his hands down on the keyboard. From the box, I could watch the change of facial expression from calm acknowledgement of the audience's applause to the concentration a general might have the moment before ordering attack.

He played very well. It was compelling, though Richard looked bored with the music. He had insisted that we not meet during the interval. Melinda, typically, showed no reaction to anything, but applauded with the rest of us. Given her total detachment, it was hard to speak to her, and all her responses were monosyllabic.

"I never said, but I think the portrait is excellent," I said to her.

She nodded.

"Yes it is."

Then she added, "Erich is a genius. I'm afraid Richard is no match for him."

The lights went down and the second half began. The music was very loud, atonal and abstract. Though modern, it was not unpleasing. The ovation was thunderous. I'm no expert but I didn't expect Gaunt would have any problem with the critics tomorrow.

He walked back and forth to the piano again and again. While acknowledging the applause, he stopped, mid-bow. He stared at Richard then looked towards us. He glared at me, then staring again at Richard, he backed to the bench and sat down.

The applause swelled, then dropped off to a hush. The lights went down again.

Gaunt began to play. I looked at Melinda.

"It's the Toccata and Fantasia," she whispered urgently.

I watched her throughout the piece.

Melinda sat rigidly as the notes rang out, and at the conclusion of the Toccata, she had the look of someone in shock.

I looked towards Richard who, for the first time, seemed caught up by the music.

The Fantasia began, and as it progressed, I thought Melinda looked more relaxed and calm, but when it finished, I saw that I had misunderstood everything as Melinda slumped forwards and lay still on the floor of the box.

Like poor Lizzie, she knew what was happening, but thought it a worthwhile way to spend her life.

Gower

Thoughts and Whispers

Gower

There's one in nearly every class. One whose eyes are out the window, whose mind is somewhere else, and who appears to have few friends.

Yet, these students, too, fall into different categories. There are those who are not unexpectedly vacant, who didn't hear the question, who write next to nothing, and reveal little of themselves, mainly because there is so little to reveal. And then, there are those who, when they do look at you, startle you with the *knowing* in their eyes.

Rachel Gower was in the latter category.

Definitely.

She defined it.

I was teaching in a convent. Not the usual place to find me, but they needed a head of English to introduce the new GCSE examinations, and my predecessor had seen enough changes to the examination system in her career and chose to retire. Overall, I don't think it was a particularly good school, not because of bad teaching but because it didn't foster aspirations. It was, as the chairman of the governors and Mother Superior said, a school for good Catholic wives and mothers.

This was 1987, forsooth.

Long after the school's closure – the ancient nuns had discovered that the land was worth millions and would keep them in worry-free retirement, and looking out from their Victorian pile on a few rows of ticky-tacky houses would be less of an inconvenience than running a school – I kept in touch with a number of staff and a few girls for a couple of decades.

But there are certain students that teachers remember.

Forever.

Lest anyone fall for the common but wholly inaccurate view that teaching at an English convent boarding school is some sort of male fantasy land, one thing is certain: they have never been in a steamy classroom with thirty fifteen-year-old girls after games. That and the unforgiving malice that swirls around like a green miasma are enough to banish impure thoughts even from non-Catholics – and we haven't got to the other seductive and alluring characteristics like hair and school jackets that reek of cigarette smoke or weed; the appalling language; the Gorgonesque stares; the sublime sulks of the French girls; or the incomprehensible verbal assaults of the aristocratic Spanish *señoritas* that reduce their victims (often their siblings) to wailing lumps of jelly; the fug of forbidden hairspray, and upset bottles of nail varnish in their desks.

What a piece of work, as someone said.

Still, they all looked beautiful lined up in the pews in Chapel, and their singing could be sublime.

∽

The school was built in 1898 as a single, large building with a long chapel on the ground floor along with the refectory, kitchens and a few offices. On the first floor were the classrooms, and the top floor and attics housed the dormitories.

In the next decade, the school expanded and a large and unexpectedly beautiful gothic-style chapel was built. It was constructed from stones gathered night after night by a crocodile of nuns from the shingle beach at the foot of the hill.

One result was that the old chapel was subdivided into three classrooms. The corner classroom, furthest from the old altar, was mine. It had minimal adornments: a dado rail and a modest coving. The windows which had been translucent were now clear, and I had a spectacular view of the Channel and the Devon coast – on the days it was visible.

However, between the time my room was part of the chapel and its conversion to a classroom, it served as an emergency hospital during the Great War.

When I discovered this, I asked if there were any pictures. There were a few of when it was the chapel, then ones of the room full of beds crisply made and awaiting patients, and then one or two of the room in the process of being cleared. A few of my students insisted that some the beds were still in the dormitories.

There were also pictures of patients on the adjacent lawn and gardens (now tennis courts), sitting in the sun, talking to visitors, or enjoying a cigarette or a pipe.

❧

As at many struggling independent schools, I was asked to teach both English and History. I didn't mind. I had been teaching long enough to be able to manage time and preparation and as no one knew the demands of the new GCSEs, I was at no particular disadvantage.

What teaching both subjects did mean was that I saw my students (I'll let the epithet, "my girls," remain firmly enclosed in another volume) more than most subject teachers saw theirs.

In the lower forms, there were five English classes each week and three in History. In the examination years, there were more. Four each for English Language and Literature, and five for History. At "A" level, there were six lessons each. This meant that for those doing both history and English at GCSE and "A" level, I spent a lot of time with the girls.

Rachel Gower was one of them.

By the Upper Sixth years, I knew a lot about my students and they knew a fair bit about me, though fiction played a significant role in my autobiography.

Maintaining a professional distance was not difficult

as the school was traditional – old fashioned – and formal by normal standards then. It would strain credibility today: Until Year 5 (GCSE year), girls were known by their surnames. In Year 5, and in the Sixth Form, they would be called "Miss X," though staff, when speaking of a girl, would continue to use their surname. Girls would stand quietly when a teacher entered the room. In the lower forms, they would stand when called on to speak.

Within the context of the school, this was accepted as perfectly normal, even in 1987.

I got to know backgrounds, holiday destinations and activities, boyfriends, future plans, favourite foods, pop and film stars, and their latest best friends at schools. I learned their attitudes towards their parents, siblings, politics, religion, fashion, and sex. None of this was directly shared with me, but through normal chatter and occasional comments about characters and plots. Essays might also occasionally stray into personal experience territory. And, of course, there was the gossip and the rumours they spread.

I came to know most of these girls better than their parents did, but I learned next to nothing about Rachel Gower.

In her first years at the school, Gower was teased, and I dare say, bullied, by her peers for being quiet, self-reliant and limited in her socialising. Somehow, she held her own and by the end of her second year, she had established herself, having earned respect from her performance in tennis, lacrosse, and good academic work.

Gower earned mostly "B"s in English and History with the odd "A". In Mathematics, it was reversed. At GCSE, her best subjects were maths and the sciences, yet she had chosen to study English, History and Mathematics at "A" level, an unusual combination.

The head of science was angry with her for those choices – this was not a school where teachers were simply disappointed. The careers' teacher had despaired of any long-term planning from Gower as she had announced that she did not plan on going to university – where she would have done very well.

In English and History, her reluctance to speak much or join class discussions was a factor in keeping her from the top marks, but her writing became detailed, penetrating and well-reasoned. It did not surprise me that she quietly moved towards the top of the class.

I knew little of her background. Student files were not available to teachers in those days. Over time, I learned that her mother was dead and that her father was in "government service."

This phrase didn't arouse any curiosity in the nuns or most of the other members of staff, but one day over lunch, I found that I was not the only one to have suspicions.

Strictly speaking, Miss Noakes should have retired. If she was not over seventy, she was very near to it. She had been a maths teacher at the school since the late forties and never aspired to anything more than teach and raise dahlias in the walled garden of her small house a short distance from the convent.

Miss Noakes was a good colleague. She was supportive and would advise younger members of staff how to handle the eccentricities of the nuns, and her knowledge of the ability and performance of the girls was exceptional. She was professionally friendly, but, like Rachel Gower, gave little about herself away.

In my six years at the school, I did manage to glean a few interesting bits of information about Miss Noakes. She had earned a first in Mathematics at Oxford and on graduation had joined GCHQ where she remained for the duration of the war. She had, allegedly, worked with the top code-breakers and was a contributor to Turing's work.

Forty years later, she was still completing the *Times* crossword in the staff room in less than eight minutes.

It was during the mid-year exams when Gower was in the Lower Sixth, that Miss Noakes had raised the subject of Gower over lunch. We had both been on lunch duty and were eating later than the girls and colleagues, so were alone in the refectory.

"Have you looked at Miss Gower's paper yet?" she asked.

"Not in detail. She wrote at length and appears to have quoted a number of sources," I said.

"Interesting girl," Miss Noakes said, then paused. "Not many do English, History and Mathematics. Do you have any insight into her plans?"

I shook my head.

There were opportunities for casual chat, usually before break, lunch or at the end of the day. Girls would hang behind to talk with friends, put away their work, or ask questions. I would usually stay until the room cleared, or at least until there were only one or two stragglers, or girls who had decided to continue working in the room.

This was a time when they might ask questions about work, exams, or make a comment about something unrelated to just about everything else. Notably, while teaching at a boys' school, a Fourth Form boy came up to me after class, and asked, *á propos* of nothing, "Do you know what Betjeman's favourite London terminus is? *Broad Street.* I ask you, Broad Street!" then wandered away.

Girls were little different, though their comments were seldom about railways.

Such exchanges were often about disputed grades,

homework, lost property, a perceived slight from another girl or teacher, or some other piece of "unfairness."

Unless problems were serious, these post-lesson exchanges were usually only a few sentences: "What are you doing this weekend?" "Did Miss Fitchett ever find her bananas?" "Have you finished your UCCA form?" "What universities are you looking at?" "Have you passed your driver's test yet?"

For me, it was a perfect time to ask, "What are your plans for next year?" It was casual, and there was no problem asking it when other girls were still in the room.

"I'm going to look after my father," Gower said.

It was not the reply I expected. I tried not to look surprised.

"Where is he?"

"He's in Virginia now, but he moves around a lot. It will be fun to travel."

"Will this be a gap year?"

She shrugged.

"We'll see," she said before leaving for lunch.

∽

It wasn't much to go on, but it was more than Miss Noakes had managed to glean.

"Like you, I've never tried to pry too much – especially with this one," Miss Noakes said. "I listen, offer advice, and answer questions. I don't try to push them but rather plant seeds."

"How clever do you think Gower is?" I asked.

She shook her head.

"Hard to tell," she replied. "I don't think she pushes herself. Very little seems to really engage her."

That was true. I'd never known her to have a passion for anything and said so.

"All girls have phases and fads," Miss Noakes said. "Whether art, films or pop stars, sports people, or a celebrity – if we're lucky, an artist, writer or scientist – but she's had none."

"Does her father need looking after?" I asked.

"Good question," she said, thinking. "I can under-stand wanting to get to know your only parent after so long a time, but teenaged girls don't usually make it sound like their life's work. Do you know what her father does?"

"Not really."

"Neither do I," she said, shaking her head.

She appeared to be puzzling something out.

"She's only said he's in government service," she said eventually.

"I have a theory about that," I said.

Miss Noakes looked up quickly.

"Oh, yes? And, what's that?"

She was suddenly animated.

"I always hear that he's in 'government service.' Not

in the Civil Service. If he were in politics or the military, one would say so, but 'government service' starts to look like the intelligence services," I said. "Given that he's in the United States, I think that means he's either a bodyguard or in MI6. Gower says he's in Virginia, which could indicate either, but, given the pay grade necessary to send his daughter here, I think it's the latter and that he's at Langley."

I couldn't tell what Miss Noakes was thinking and laughed nervously.

"You're the GCHQ graduate; you tell me, am I way off base?" I asked.

"A lot has changed since my time," she said, "but I can't fault your logic or deductions."

≈

Having said that Gower had no strong academic passions, about halfway through her Lower Sixth year, she developed a strong interest in the World War I writers. She loved Wilfred Owen's poetry, and read *Good-bye to All That, A Farewell to Arms, Memoirs of a Fox-hunting Man,* as well as other writers.

The interest continued into her Upper Sixth year when she wrote some outstanding detailed essays.

When the detail began to overshadow the literary work and the actual answer to the question was getting lost, I asked her to talk to me formally.

She seemed to have little idea why I wanted to speak

with her, and was surprised that I didn't like some of the detail she included.

"Miss Gower, this essay is very good. The idea of comparing and contrasting the experience of gas in 'Dulce et Decorum Est' with Trotter's story about the May tree in *Journey's End* is excellent," I began.

"Thank you."

"However, you move away from the main point of the essay and spend time talking about the different gases and their smells and effects. I'm not sure where the information is coming from, it's not from the poem or play."

"I thought additional information would help," she said.

Her manner was without emotion. She wasn't arguing, she didn't even seem disappointed with my comments.

"You have two pages about the works and three pages about tear gas, chlorine gas, phosgene gas, and mustard gas. Don't you think this is over-kill, if you will excuse the expression," I asked.

"But it's true, isn't it?"

"This is a literature exam, not a chemistry exam, or even a history exam."

She looked at me with her dark unfathomable eyes but said nothing.

"Where are you getting this information from?" I

asked. "I'm not saying it's not accurate, but I don't think any of it is in any book in this school's library."

She moved as if to begin a protest, but I went on.

"For example, you mention that chlorine gas shells were painted green and mustard gas shells, yellow. This is pretty specialist – even arcane – knowledge."

Then, a thought struck me.

"Is this information coming from your father?" I asked.

"No," she answered quickly. "He never writes."

"Then where is it from?"

But she was looking out the window towards the old garden.

"All right, Miss Gower," I said. "All I'm saying is that you have the chance of doing extremely well as long as you stick to answering the question and not rambling through long superfluous technical detail. Let me know if I can help."

"Thank you, sir."

There wasn't a hint of a smile, relief, or even boredom.

I showed the essay to Miss Noakes.

"Do you know where she might be getting this information?" I asked her.

"I remember hearing about the coloured shells," she said, trying to place the source.

"It's certainly not in any of the books she's read –

even in the wider reading that I know about."

"This is a good paper until she gets into gas categories."

There were no such digressions in her work on the Tudors and Stuarts. I had dreaded long passages about torture devices, but her work there was very good – and normal.

The weeks towards exams were passing. Girls were becoming either more focused or just giving up and swanning about pretending they didn't care. A few we got back on track telling them that giving up looked worse to employers and colleges of further education than "C"s and "D"s.

Gower was working steadily. She seemed to be working in my classroom more often and for longer. I didn't mind. We stayed out of each other's way apart from friendly greetings. Her work still had flashes of detail, but it was now relevant to her arguments and evidence.

One day in March, I'd been at a play rehearsal and went to collect homework books from my classroom. I found Gower there. She was at her desk, her books open.

"Don't be late for supper," I said, walking to my desk.

I wasn't paying much attention to her until I heard a choked, "No, sir."

I looked up and saw she'd been crying.

"Can I help with anything?"

It was cowardly and callous thing to say, but it was what teachers were being driven to.

She shook her head and began to gather her things.

"Has someone hurt you? Been mean?"

She shook her head.

"Bad news from home?"

This actually provoked a smile.

"No," she said, regaining her normal manner. "All's fine there."

I nodded and she left.

Such behaviour at a girls' boarding school isn't unusual. Also, the students in the examination years tend to be stressed and more sensitive to – well, to just about everything.

෴

The French teacher, Madame Franzen, wanted to stage *Phèdre* as the school play that year. While she had strong views on what the production should look like, she had little idea about blocking movements, directing, or helping girls with projection.

I agreed to help, though I would have preferred to see a production of *Charlie's Aunt*, *The Importance of Being Earnest*, *Harvey*, *Arsenic and Old Lace*, or just about anything but this creaky festival of misery. Ironically, my hardest job was to keep it from being laughable.

We didn't do it in French. It might have been easier if we had done. The subtleties of the French were lost and the English suggested that it had been translated not *into* English, but *out* of French. Like every other decision in this production, it was out of my hands; all I had to do was make it work.

Madame Franzen busied herself with what she considered the *mise et scene*, which was set design, painting and lighting. For some reason, she thought Van Gogh-style rooms would lend themselves to a representation of ancient Troezen, Peloponnesus.

What ever it would be, it would never be the masterpiece of the human mind of Voltaire's opinion. My objective was simply getting through to the end with an audience still more or less there, and not laughing too hard.

I have to say, the cast was good and seemed to sense the reality of things. This worked in my favour as none of them wanted to be responsible for a descent into chaos, or worse, farce, and made a real effort to make it work.

With *Phèdre* occupying so much time and space in my mind, my work for my classes was confined to the lessons and marking, and things were just about being held together.

Then, on the day before the dress rehearsal, Miss

Noakes came to me after a technical run-through. (Everyone had great fun trying to mix the sounds of wounded horned monsters thrashing about with that of terrified horses, wrecked chariots and Hippolytus being dragged to his death. For many of them, knowing how the sounds were made would elicit hilarity rather than cathartic pathos.)

"May I have a word," Miss Noakes said, appearing at the door to the school hall as I prepared to leave.

She held a sheaf of papers.

"Julia showed me this and after reading it, I thought I have a word with you, given our last conversation," she said.

Julia Maynard was my predecessor in the English department. Although retired, she acted as clerk to the governing body and continued to edit the school's annual magazine *De Verbis et Veritate*, commonly known as *V&V*. I had heard that Miss Maynard had known Miss Noakes at GCHQ and, after the war, they had both come to the school.

"Gower submitted a story that – well, read it. It's not long."

She handed me three sheets and we walked into the staff room where I sat down and read.

Miss Noakes sat silently as I read the pages of feint lined paper with Gower's very legible but eccentric handwriting.

Thoughts and Whispers

It was a short story that used her study of the literature of the Great War as its setting. It was a fairly simple tale of a soldier from the Herefordshire countryside who ends up at the second Battle of Arras in April 1917. The descriptions of the front, the action and the reactions of the men were recognisable from Sassoon, Graves and Sheriff. Then, I could perceive the reason for Miss Noakes's reaction when I read about the creeping barrage in preparation for the attack and the demolition of the German's barbed wire using eighteen-pounder shells with the new French No. 106 fuse.

I glanced up at Miss Noakes, who merely nodded as if to say, "Read on."

I read on and came to a description of the wounded country lad whose left arm was shattered and subsequently amputated by a pistol shot from a Luger P.08 using a 278F 123-grain truncated-nose bullet.

The soldier was later sent to recover at a facility on the Devon coast but ultimately died of infections while there.

I set the pages down, but did not look at Miss Noakes.

As a story, it was very accomplished. The final scenes in what was obviously the convent was a very neat trick and showed a mature use of personal experience. But the detail of the weapons –

"Who has Gower been talking to?" I asked, looking up.

320

Miss Noakes looked at me with a grim Cassandra-like intensity.

"I think you know."

I met her eyes and stayed focused on them, trying to decipher what she was really saying. Finally, I thought I understood.

"This has happened before?"

She nodded, ominously.

&

My troubles with *Phèdre* faded to nothing in the face of what now confronted me, yet, I had to continue my normal work.

Curiously, the distraction of Gower and her soldier gave me a better perspective on the play and, now in company of more powerful forces, I was able to relax at the dress rehearsal. The girls seemed to sense my loss of stress and responded better than I could have expected.

The dress rehearsal and the two performances proceeded with remarkable smoothness. The set jarred with the action, but the sound effects the girls had come up with got a round of applause on the second night, which prepared the way for Phèdre's final confession which was as good as it could get given the clunky translation.

It was, of course, Madame Franzen who was singled out by the headmistress during the curtain calls, and Madame Franzen who received the bouquet.

While Madame Franzen spoke with parents and visitors, the girls gave me a very funny card which they had drawn and signed. It would last longer and mean more than any roses.

⁓

A week later when the magazine came out and the production of *Phèdre* dismantled (guess who had to deal with tearing down the set, storing the bits, returning the props and costumes and putting away the makeup that hadn't gone walkies), the exams were about to begin.

Sixth form girls were able to study in their rooms, the library, empty classrooms, and when the weather was nice, in the grounds. Consequently, I didn't see much of them, and was besieged by girls doing GCSE who wanted reassurance, answers to last minute questions and the whole year's course taught in half an hour.

I was in my classroom, marking work from the other classes in the time between morning break and lunch. Exams were going on, and the final English exam was that afternoon. I wanted to be there in case any of the girls had last-minute questions.

I had just finished talking to one, explaining something to do with the rubric – which I took as an excuse to get a bit of reassurance – when Gower came in.

She said hello and asked if she could work at her desk.

As she sat down and started getting out her books, I

held up the copy of the magazine.

"That's a very good story, Miss Gower," I said.

"Thank you," she said, without smiling.

"I wouldn't have thought you knew so much about munitions," I said as casually as I could.

She didn't flinch.

"It's amazing what one picks up," she said, and opened her notebook.

We worked in silence for half an hour or so and then the second exam of the morning ended and it was time for lunch.

I collected my things and was walking out of the room when I heard Gower whisper sharply.

"No! He'll think I'm bonkers."

I resisted turning around, but when I went to the staff table in the refectory, Miss Noakes looked at me and came over.

"You look like you've seen. . . something unexpected," she said in a wry way.

She sat down opposite me.

"Does it show?"

"What did you see?"

"Nothing. It's what I heard."

She listened as I told her of our short conversation and what I'd heard on the way out.

"That's so often the way," Miss Noakes said, shaking her head. "Absolutely nothing to go on."

"What can you tell me? How often does this happen? Is it always in that room? That's been my room since I came to the school. I've never had an indication of – *anything*."

My questions and words rushed out, but Miss Noakes seemed unsurprised.

"It's adolescent girls," she said. "They attract – well, curious things."

I chuckled, more at the way she said it than anything else.

"Gower is hardly adolescent. She's eighteen."

Miss Noakes raised her hand.

"Exactly. Gower probably began seeing, or hearing – things – soon after she got here," she said. "You've taught her for a number of years, haven't you?"

"First year, third, fifth, and Lower and Upper Sixth," I said.

"History and English," Miss Noakes added. "See. Gower would have spent a lot of time in the room. It's why she studies there, too."

I looked at the clever lady.

"You knew, didn't you?" I challenged her.

"I – *suspected*," she replied. "As you have discovered, there's not much to go on. Nothing you can see or hear. Just those tantalising unexplained bits of knowledge and detail. I always expected to get a slight smell of something. Gas, pears, bleach, pipe tobacco, antiseptic.

Something."

She shrugged.

"Nothing in forty years," she continued. "You'd think his power would have faded in nearly seventy years, but it appears to be undiminished."

"How many girls have you suspected?"

"Only four. One can never be sure. There's no way of knowing how many he started with but who either left the school, or never had lessons in that room again," Miss Noakes said. "I'm afraid that it's likely that Gower chose History and English more for the room than any love for the subjects – or you."

That wasn't flattering. Professionally or personally.

"Do you know if the – *experience* – affected their later life?" I asked. "Was there any lasting consequence?"

She raised both hands to show she had no idea.

"If they'd been having regular contact with him, what was it like to suddenly lose it?" I asked.

"I know that none of the ones I suspected ever came back to visit, but not a great number of girls do. That's more for reasons of distance than anything, but I never saw those four, and don't ever expect to see Gower again."

&

Miss Noakes's remark was more prescient than I could have imagined, for when I came into school in the morning, one of the girls said that the headmistress wanted to see me.

I expected her to ask about the previous day's English examination, and possibly the status of the GCSE coursework submissions or moderations.

The less said about the headmistress the better, apart from noting that she was one of the major reasons the school closed. Communication was not her *forté*, and once in a staff committee meeting, someone wondered what was.

"Miss Gower's father arrived at the school last night, paid her remaining expenses and collected his daughter," she said, without a hello or good morning. "I have asked the housemistress to gather her things from the dormitory. If you can clear her desk and anything that's in your classroom, or the mathematics room, the bursar will bundle them and ship them to her."

"To Virginia?" I asked.

The headmistress had spoken to me from her desk while reviewing some other papers, but now she looked up.

"To Kinross," she said, then looked back down at her desk.

As I left, I heard her mutter, "Virginia? The idea!"

I had my normal classes that morning, so it wasn't until after lunch that I began to pick through the piles of papers on the classroom shelves, extracting Gower's papers. I was about to start on her desk when Miss

Noakes came in with an empty cardboard box.

"I thought you could use this," she said.

"I gather you had to collect her things from the maths' room."

"Who else?" she said as we walked to Gower's desk.

I slid the odd book about to get a measure of what was in there. The school didn't have desk inspections, so all manner of things could be found. Most common were food (including chewing gum), fan magazines, cigarettes, makeup, endless tissues, and religious clobber (rosaries, medals, Mass cards, devotional leaflets, missionary appeals, and the like, handed out by visiting speakers). Just about everything was possible: hair clips, combs and brushes (occasionally a can of hairspray); gloves, nylon tights, postcards, letters, pictures of boys (some laminated illicitly in the Art Room or preserved in Sellotape), and the general detritus of stationery stores: sharpeners, pencil cases or boxes, rubbers, clips, staples, gummed labels and so on. Needless to say, all of the latter were branded with some popstar's image or name, or brightly coloured pattern. You could imagine parents and relatives sending them to their daughters and nieces, or putting them in their stockings at Christmas. No doubt, the occasional one was half-inched on an outing, too. More usually found in the dormitories (so I was told) were aspirin, paracetamol, Feminax, vitamins, appetite suppressants and Senocot.

One year, there was something of a sensation in a staff meeting when one of the nuns produced a pair of bright red four-inch stilettos with ankle straps that had been found in the desk of a fourth-year girl called Higgins.

Sister Mary Polycarp described her shock at finding them, at finding them in this school, at finding them in her classroom, at finding them in this girl's desk; a girl that had hood-winked everyone into believing her to be virtuous and kind; who had demonstrated great promise, but who obviously had now put her school career – not to mention her soul – in danger. . . .

In terms of fire and brimstone, Sister Mary Polycarp's diatribe was a solid 9/10. It was impossible to interrupt her and it continued for a full seven minutes, after which the nearly apoplectic lady sat down, shaking. Water and tissues were fetched.

The headmistress then launched into a social commentary, lasting nearly as long, that finished with her plans to summon the girl and tell her to pack her things.

There was silence that followed when many of us considered whether we had slipped a century or two. It was ended by a soft voice.

"Headmistress, if I might say something?"

It was Miss Cross, who taught a range of things that had disappeared from most schools: speaking and debating, deportment, etiquette, household management, dress-making, elocution and drama. It was as the drama teacher that she demonstrated her not inconsiderable credentials and skill, and her lower school productions were outstanding.

"I hardly think there is anything to be added," the headmistress said, shortly.

"I rather think there is, Headmistress."

This was one of the occasions when Miss Cross exercised her talents. Her voice made the headmistress's commentary and plans for Higgins sound feeble.

"Those shoes," she began, standing up and walking to the headmistress and removing the shoes from before her, "come from the school's costume wardrobe."

At least two suppressed sniggers could be heard.

"Higgins is wearing them for her mock GCSE Drama practical next week when performing a *prescribed* text. I lent them to her so she could get more comfortable wearing them, as the time she has them on in the lesson is insufficient for a girl – *who has no experience wearing such things* – to get the hang of them. For the record, all she has said about them is to complain.

"Sister Mary Polycarp has made an honest mistake, and jumped to an unfortunate conclusion," Miss Cross concluded. "So, after this meeting, I shall take the shoes downstairs and return them to Higgins' desk."

If the rest of us were waiting for further retribution,

we were disappointed. The headmistress looked around the table, wearing the innocent expression of one who might have just walked into the meeting, and said, "Item One."

Against this background, it was with some uneasiness that Miss Noakes and I opened Gower's desk.

The girl appeared to be a minimalist. There was a pencil case of a tartan pattern. It contained a dozen pencils of different colours and a few biros. There was a ruler, and a neat maths' set containing: a pair of compasses, dividers, protractor, triangles, a French curve. There was a plastic box of paper clips. We removed these and placed them on a nearby desk.

Next were her notebooks, several spiral bound and a ring binder. There were some text books, a pad of graph paper, and a copy of Wilson's *What Happens in Hamlet,* and one old copy of *The Face.* Her essays were in her ring binder, but there were several sheets of outlines for trial questions for both History and English.

"Doesn't tell us much about her, does it?" Miss Noakes asked. "No college catalogues; no careers information."

"Nothing about the United States, either," I said.

We put the books and stationery bits into the cardboard box with the other papers I'd collected earlier.

"Ah," I said and went to my desk. "I'll put this in, too."

It was a copy of *V&V*.

"She should keep a copy of that."

While Miss Noakes was arranging the articles in the box containing the school career of Rachel Gower, I slipped my fingers into all four corners of the desk before closing the lid.

I drew out a small grey object and held it up.

"Oh, my!" Miss Noakes exclaimed.

I turned it in my fingers.

"I'm not an expert, but I'd say that was a 123-grain truncated-nose bullet."

The End

By the same author:

Nantucket Summer
Wachusett
The Camels of the Qur'an
Portland Place
The Countess Comes Home
On the Edge of Dreams and Nightmares
Entrusted in Confidence
Undivulged Crimes
Lost Lady
The Rock Pool
Ardmore Endings

Printed in Great Britain
by Amazon